THE PORN STAR MURDERS

a thriller

VICTOR METHOS

Even in the centuries which appear to us to be the most mon-strous and foolish, the immortal appetite for beauty has always found satisfaction.

—Charles Baudelaire

Beauty and folly are old companions.

—Benjamin Franklin

CHAPTER 1

San Diego, California. May 19, 2006

T he room screamed as Detective Jon Stanton turned on the lights.

Blood was everywhere, coating carpets and walls and the fan that dangled from the ceiling. It was spattered randomly in places—an arterial spray that made him think of the paintings of Jackson Pollock—but in other places it held the outlines of bodies. Bodies of the family that had been stacked against the wall like meat left over from a hunt.

Stanton stepped inside but had to lean against the doorframe. He covered his ears with his hands, as if the screams in his head were real, and had to wait a few moments before he could remove them.

He walked to the middle of the room in front of the large bed with the white canopy, as the booties covering his shoes crackled like paper.

Mike Blum and his two children had been placed against the far wall, sitting, in an upright position. The responding officers had found their hands bound with duct tape. Stanton turned to the bed where Mrs. Nina Blum had been found. That was where the monster had spent most of his time; she was the one he had come for.

Stanton wished he could've been here before the bodies

were removed by the Medical Examiner's Office, but officially, this was his partner's case. He hadn't heard the messages to get down here until five in the morning when he'd woken to go surfing.

His partner swaggered in behind him. Stanton turned to him and saw that he wore designer jeans with a Ralph Lauren leather jacket. No matter where he was, Eli Sherman always looked like he was on a date.

"Sorry I couldn't get here sooner," Stanton said.

"No worries," Sherman said, leaning against the wall. "Quite a mess, isn't it? I don't think I've had one of these in years."

Stanton knew he was referring to a DPK: a disorganized-personality killer. As opposed to an organized-personality killer, the disorganized killer was full of rage and took no precautions. Victims were chosen at random, on a whim, and then subjected to a nightmare they could never have imagined. Luckily, the rage caused the DPK to kill quickly, and the victims' suffering wasn't prolonged. Afterward, the corpses would become the center of attention.

"I have the crime scene unit's video and photos whenever you're ready to look at them. The male subject and the children were shot. One round in the back of the head. Quickest way to kill, so he wanted to take them out first."

"He wasn't here for them," Stanton said.

"I don't know why he leaned them up against the wall, though. Maybe he just needed to get the bodies out of the way so he could work on the female subject."

Stanton hated the way Sherman referred to victims as "subjects." They had been dehumanized before death, and Stanton felt they owed them the courtesy not to do it after death. But he didn't say anything. Every detective had his own way of dealing with the horror.

"No," Stanton said, "that's not what it is."

"What then?"

"He wanted an audience. He leaned them up against the wall so they could watch. But he wanted them dead first. He couldn't perform in front of them if they were still living."

Sherman was quiet a moment. "Careful what you do with that laser perception, Jon. Point it in the wrong place and you might see things you don't want to see."

"Hey, guys," a forensic tech from CSU said as he poked his head in, "we got cameras outside. One of you want to give them the 'no comment'?"

"You do it," Sherman said. "I'll diagram and then get outta here."

Stanton turned and began to follow the tech out. He glanced back once and saw Sherman standing next to the bed, deep red and black stains where Mrs. Blum had lain. Gently, he ran his fingers across the sheets and mumbled something to himself. Stanton would have to ask him later what it was.

CHAPTER 2

Present Day

Jon Stanton walked into his office suite at Diamond View Tower. The offices were plush, the furniture imported leather with a flatscreen in the waiting room. Diamond View was one of the most expensive office buildings in the city. After Stanton had quit the San Diego PD, he wasn't sure if becoming a private investigator would even pay his rent.

But he had a reputation, only a glimmer of which he was aware of when he was with the PD, of being able to solve cases and find people that no one else could. Missing persons cases lined up to hire him once word got out that he was on his own. Within one month, he had to begin turning clients away and could now charge whatever he wanted.

His secretary, Jill, greeted him with a Post-it Note that said his ten o'clock appointment was running a few minutes late and he walked into his office and threw it in the trash. He looked out of his floor-to-ceiling windows onto Petco Park Stadium. A college baseball team was there now, practicing. He watched them a long time before Jill buzzed him.

"Yeah, Jill?"

"Toys for Tots called. They wanted to thank you for the donations."

"I dropped those off anonymously. How'd they know it was me?"

"You've done it for twelve years, Jon. And you're probably the only person that does it in the summer. I think they know.

And Mrs. Anna Dopler is here."

"Send her in please."

Stanton sat down behind his cherry wood desk as a middle-aged woman in a tight blouse and high heels walked in.

"How are you, Detective?" she said, holding out her hand.

Stanton stood and shook it before sitting back down. "It's just Jon now."

Anna Dopler sat down across from him and exhaled. She glanced at the wall decorations: Stanton's PhD in Psychology from the University of Utah, photos of him at various vacation spots, some awards from the American Psychological Association.

"You don't have anything up from your days as a cop," she said.

"That's perceptive of you. No, I don't."

"My husband, well, ex-husband, was a cop. He tried to forget about it too when he left."

"What is it I can do for you, Mrs. Dopler?"

"Yeah, sorry, I know you're busy. It's my son. He's been missing for over eight months now, and the detective at Missing Persons said they can't help me anymore. That they're putting the case in the Open-Unsolved Unit and from there it'll be closed and archived if they can't come up with any new leads."

"How old is your son?"

"Fourteen, now."

"When was the last time you saw him?"

"Like I said, it was eight months ago. He was going to take the bus to a friend's house that evening. I was…I was busy at the time and I couldn't take him. So he had to take the bus. He never showed up to his friend's house. No one saw him on the bus."

Stanton took out a legal pad and scribbled a few notes. "Where's his father?"

"His father and I have a…complicated relationship. We have an open marriage. He was busy at the time too."

Stanton realized what she meant by open: they were swingers. Like most swingers, the sex probably turned to obsession and addiction. Afterward, the marriage and attention to the children began to fade.

"What has Missing Persons said?"

"They looked into all his friends. He was a good kid, Detective. He wasn't into drugs or anything like that. He didn't have anyone in his life that would have taken him from us."

"Did they have any suspects?"

"No." She took something out of her purse and slid it across the desk. It was a controller to a video game console.

"What's this?"

"It's his. He's the only one who ever played it. I was told that I should bring something personal of his to you."

"Who told you that?"

"I was recommended to you by a friend."

Stanton slid the controller back. "Mrs. Dopler, I am not psychic. There is no such thing as extrasensory perception. No valid studies have corroborated any of it."

"But I was told—"

"I know, and I'm sorry you were misled. I don't know how I got that reputation, but it's not true. I don't do anything differently than the police. All the evidence is there, you just have to look."

"I researched you, Detective. I wouldn't have come here otherwise. I know how many cases you solve, what the people in the police force thought of you. I'm not stupid."

"I'm not saying—"

"Jon?" Jill's voice came through his phone.

"Yes, Jill."

"I have Lieutenant Daniel Childs here whenever you're done."

"Thanks."

An image flashed in Stanton's mind. It was of him and Childs when Daniel had learned that Stanton was quitting the force for good. They were standing on a beach near La Jolla, Stanton wet after having just come out of the ocean, Childs in an Armani suit. Childs had looked so desperate, pleading with him not to leave.

Stanton couldn't understand why and he still didn't.

"Mrs. Dopler, I'll be happy to look into your son's disappearance but there're some ground rules: first, you'll need to be completely open and honest with me no matter how uncomfortable it makes you. Second, there're going to be documents, like his medical records, that only you as his mother can get. When I ask you to get those documents, you have to get them for me as quickly as possible. Third, you can never bring up this psychic business again."

She nodded. "Okay. I promise."

"Jill will have an intake sheet for you. I'll call you once I've gotten the police reports, and we'll go through the details. I'll need to come out and visit the house to look at your son's room, if you've left it intact."

"We have. Whatever you need. He's my only son, Detective. I'm too old now to have another."

"I understand. I'll do everything I can."

They stood and shook hands again before she walked out. Stanton noticed a bite mark on the upper part of her thigh, revealed by the slit in her skirt. In an instant, he could see her son. He tried his best not to reach any conclusions at the beginning of a case, but he knew already that he was dead. Swinger parties draw sexual deviants. Many men hire prostitutes to pose as their wives in order to get into them. As the sexual addiction escalates, only more and more graphic and deviant behavior satisfies. Pedophilia and sadism are two of the extreme behaviors that recovering sex addicts, almost exclusively male, report after prolonged addiction.

Anna Dopler had brought madness into her life and she had paid the price for it.

Stanton looked out to the practice at the stadium again. He watched a young man bunt and sprint to first base so fast he almost tripped and fell.

"Send in the lieutenant," Stanton said as he pressed the com button on his phone.

Daniel Childs had bulked up even more. Now in his forties,

his dark black skin appeared smoother and tighter than it had in his thirties. His forehead was clear of any wrinkles and his soft green eyes were covered by designer eyeglasses. But just as he had in his thirties, he still preferred tight shirts that showed off his arms.

Childs smiled as he slapped hands with Stanton and brought him near, bumping shoulders with him.

"How you been, Jon?"

"Good. Great. You look bigger."

"Just clean livin' and heavy liftin', man. I've gotten into powerlifting recently. Got my first meet in two months up in Long Beach."

"That's great, Danny. A man your age should try to get out more."

He smirked. "Smart ass."

Stanton sat down as Childs did the same.

"What brings you downtown?"

Childs turned his cell phone to vibrate. "Business, man. Got something I wanted to talk to you about. I didn't want to bug you at home."

Stanton said, "You can stop by anytime," but he was actually glad Childs hadn't come by. He never took his work home anymore and he preferred it that way.

"Appreciate it but I wouldn't wanna think about this shit at home. Might ruin it for me. Sometimes you don't got a choice, though. Anyway, this is what I came here for."

Childs turned on the iPad he had under his arm and opened a file. He handed it to Stanton. It was a police file, a murder book. All the documents in a murder investigation were categorized and prioritized in a file, with all the photos and videos at the end. Nowadays, many departments used electronic files, something Stanton had never grown accustomed to.

Stanton looked at the name in the upper left-hand corner: Nina Blum.

"You remember her?" Childs said.

"Yeah, I remember."

Images of a blood-stained room flooded Stanton's mind. The visit to the morgue was the most difficult part. The Blums had two children: boys. A .32 caliber round had entered each of their skulls just above the cerebellum and had exited above the eyebrows.

"It sat in the Open-Unsolved Unit for half a decade after what happened with Sherman."

Eli Sherman. The name churned Stanton's stomach. He'd been his partner for over a year before Stanton had discovered panties from two missing girls in his closet. Sherman had attempted to kill him for the discovery but failed. He was convicted of the two murders but escaped custody. His whereabouts were unknown.

For a few months afterward, Stanton would check the FBI's Ten Most Wanted list every day for updates. It took a feat of strength for him to pull himself away and detach from the thought that Sherman was still out there, somewhere, probably doing exactly what he had been doing before.

"You all right?" Childs said.

"Yeah," Stanton said, snapping back.

"Not the best memories for me either."

Stanton exhaled. "We had to abandon the case after Sherman's arrest. All his cases were turned over to IAD."

"I saw you had a suspect in there. What was his name?"

"Raymond Valdez. He was the lieutenant governor's son."

"No shit? Edwin Valdez?"

"He wasn't the LG at the time. He was in the state legislature. Raymond was only around twenty-two at the time of these murders. I got one interview in with him before his father hired an attorney and shut us down."

"What evidence did you have?"

"One of the Blums' neighbors reported seeing a man from San Diego Gas and Electric checking the meters and going into their backyard when they weren't home. Raymond Valdez was arrested that night on a DUI and they found a uniform, probably stolen or bought, from the power company. They let me know

THE PORN STAR MURDERS

and I came in and spoke to him when he was still drunk."

"You still think he's your man?"

"He denied everything and said he had never heard of the Blums and hadn't been in Kensington since he was a kid. No one could contradict what he was saying, so an arrest was never made. Honestly, though, I don't think IAD cared. The department was hurting so bad over Sherman, they just wanted all his cases to go away. If they made an arrest on this case, the defense attorney would've had Sherman's name in all the papers again. He could've even blamed him for the killings."

Childs nodded. "So, you don't think it was him?"

"I don't know. My gut said yes. I looked into Raymond's background. He'd been seeing a psychiatrist since he was four-years-old for behavioral problems and was kicked out of school when he eviscerated a dog on the playground. He was investigated for a rape charge on one of the maids at his house when he was fourteen, but she was deported and the DA's Office couldn't find her to testify against him."

Childs nodded again, lost in thought.

"What is it, Danny? You're clearly here for a reason, and I doubt it's to talk about Raymond Valdez."

"No it's not. It's to talk about the man that killed the Blums. He's sitting in maximum security right now, and he wants to talk to you."

CHAPTER 3

Stanton was silent a moment. "How do you know?"

"He confessed," Childs said, shifting in his seat. "Knew all the info, even the stuff that wasn't released in the papers."

"Like what?"

"He knew that Mrs. Blum had been object raped on top of being sodomized. He said the object had been a gun he found underneath the bed. We spoke to Michael Blum's brother. He told us Michael always had a gun underneath his bed. The cocksucker even knew the make and model. That was never released to the press. We didn't even know about that 'cause he took the gun with him."

Stanton felt a familiar tingling in his gut: it was excitement. Like the kind one feels at the end of a long chase.

He didn't forget about the Blums. The two boys had made sure of that. When he had quit the force, he scanned a few documents from the murder book and took them with him. Every few months, he would pull them out and spread them on a table at a coffee shop and go over every detail, hoping that something would jump out at him that he had missed before. Nothing ever did.

"Who is he?"

"Philip Oster. Got a rap as long as a novel. He's been at George Bailey for seven years now. Went on a distribution of a controlled substance charge in '06, three months after the Blums."

"Is that the only detail he has?"

"No, man. He went through the whole thing. Step by step. He scoped out their house with a uniform from the power company, broke in through a basement window, took out the kids first and dragged them into the bedroom before taking out Michael."

"How did he say Nina Blum was killed?"

"That's the only part that doesn't match the autopsy report. He says he shot her up with heroin and she overdosed."

Stanton remembered fielding the calls from people taking credit for the murders. The Blums were an average, upper-middle-class couple and nothing scared the upper-middle-class more than one of their own being brutally murdered for no apparent reason. The story had caught a lot of press, and with any story that does, the desperate and insane would call in and take credit.

The papers reported that she had died from strangulation. Something Stanton and Sherman had agreed to release in order to filter out those trying to take undue credit from those that may actually have knowledge about the murders. No one except Sherman, Stanton, Nina Blum's mother, who had given permission to release the information, and the ME knew what the actual cause of death was.

Stanton was silent a long time.

"You all right, man?"

"I'm fine, Danny. Just dredging up some things that have been buried a long time. The cause of death was overdose by heroin," he explained. "There's a second murder book that I guess IAD didn't get ahold of. We released cause of death as strangulation to filter the calls. No one should know that."

Now it was Childs that kept quiet. "Would you do me a favor? Mind meeting with him?"

Stanton shook his head. "I gave up my badge for a reason, Danny. I'm not about to go trudging back."

"I know, I know. But no one knows the case like you. I'm the one that caught this case and it'd be a huge help to have a second pair of eyes on it."

Stanton saw the slight upper curl of the lip: an inadvertent micro-expression. Childs wasn't telling him the truth.

"What are you leaving out, Danny?"

"What d'ya mean?"

"There's something you're not telling me because you think I won't do it if I know. What is it?"

Childs cleared his throat, clearly uncomfortable. "Look, I'll level with you. The guy won't talk to me. He won't talk to the DA's Office either. He told his attorney that the only person he'll talk to is you. He says if you meet with him, he'll give a full confession. Not just to the Blums, to five other murders too."

"What others?"

"Remember a few months back there was a story about that porn star that was killed?"

"Vaguely."

"Well she wasn't the first. She was number five. The other four were all blond, fake breasts, blue eyes, like Nina Blum. Unlike Nina, the other four were in porn too. I think our man got sick of the porn stars and moved over to the housewives."

"Why wasn't that in the media?"

Childs shrugged. "Porn star deaths happen all the time. Usually drug overdoses or STDs. Doesn't make the news much in this town anymore."

Stanton thought a moment. "I'm sorry, Danny. You've got everyone you need. I'd like to help you close those cases but I'm done with police work. I can't go back to thinking that way. It nearly killed me last time. And it'll never be just one confession. There'll be follow-up and interviews and gathering evidence and I'll get deeper and deeper until I can't get out. I help find kids now. I enjoy it and take only the cases I want to take."

Childs clicked the nails of his thumb and forefinger together. An annoying habit he'd had since Stanton first met him, when they were new uniforms on traffic patrol.

"There is one more thing I haven't told you: he didn't work alone. He says we've never caught his partner. That he's still here in the city. He says if we meet with him, he'll help us find him. Jon, if that sick bastard is gonna put other women through what Nina Blum went through—you can't say no. I know you. You can't say no to that."

"I'm sorry, Danny. I wouldn't even know where to start anymore. I'm saying no. Sorry."

Childs sighed and stood up. "I'm sorry too."

CHAPTER 4

Stanton left the office early in the afternoon and headed to La Jolla Shores, one of his favorite surfing spots. Not that the waves would be particularly good, but the beach was a mile-long crescent of golden sand packed with families. Stanton enjoyed watching them as he glided into shore on the water, letting his mind drift to wherever it would take him.

His own family wasn't nearby anymore. His ex-wife Melissa had remarried someone that played for the Chargers and then had been recruited by the New England Patriots, so the family had moved to Boston. His two sons, now nearly teenagers, had both said they wanted to stay with their mother. His older son, Matthew, had told him that she needed them a lot more than he did, which was probably true. But it didn't make the pain of distance any easier.

Stanton parked, and changed behind his Volvo. The wet suit hadn't fully dried since this morning and its coolness perked him up after the dreary drive from downtown. A local surf shop, Mickey's, kept a board for him in back for a small monthly fee and Stanton picked it up and headed to the ocean.

As he paddled out, he inhaled as one arm entered the water and exhaled as it rose up and the other entered. He took long deep breaths and exhaled loudly through his mouth. The deep oxygenation relaxed him and cleared his mind.

But as he caught his first wave and it began pulling him back to shore, he saw the children playing in the sand and instantly thought of the Blums. The two young boys lying on cold metal slabs with Y-shaped scars from the autopsies across their chests.

When Stanton had gone to see them at the morgue, they both had stamps on their right hands from their visit to a museum earlier that day. He had taken his sons to that same museum several times.

After only a few sets, he returned the board, and headed home.

Stanton lived on the eleventh floor of a skyrise, as close to the ocean as he could get. The building was secure and he had gotten to know every doorman on every shift. A precaution in case he ever saw someone as the doorman that shouldn't be there. It was a small paranoia that he allowed himself without too much reflection on it.

When he entered his apartment, the smell of cooking meats and vegetables hit his nostrils and he remembered he hadn't eaten in over five hours. His girlfriend, Emma Lyon, was in the kitchen with an apron that said KISS THE COOK. Stanton kissed her and picked a piece of bell pepper out of a frying pan.

"How was class?" he asked, placing the pepper in his mouth.

"Good. Half my students were asleep and the other half were on Facebook or Twitter."

"Chemistry isn't the most exciting subject."

"It is to me. Try this." She thrust a spoon with a thin red sauce into his mouth. "What d'ya think?"

"Needs some more salt but good."

"We're cutting back on your sodium, young man," she said, turning back to the oven. "Doctor's orders."

"You're a doctor of quantum chemistry. I don't think you're the kind that gets to tell me to cut down on salt." Stanton wrapped his arms around her waist and kissed her again.

"Well someone's affectionate today. Something happen at work?"

"Nothing much. Signed up a new client. Her fourteen-year-old son went missing eight months ago and Missing Persons is closing the case. How about you?"

"Just class and then grading papers. You ready to eat?"

The food was hot and spicy and Stanton, luckily, had exactly two plates. Emma liked wine with her meals, but out of respect for his Mormon beliefs, she never had alcohol around him.

They spoke of mundane things: the weather, gossip, the upcoming holidays. Emma had a way of relaxing him that no one or nothing else could achieve. By the time dinner was over, he had almost forgotten about the Blums. Almost.

Emma began cleaning up. "Do you want to watch a movie before I leave?" He nodded and went into the bedroom to change. After getting into shorts and a T-shirt, he reached up to the top shelf of his closet and pulled down some red file folders. Three of them. He took out the bottom one, labeled BLUM, MICHAEL AND NINA and headed out to his balcony, knowing Emma would still be busy cleaning up.

An ocean breeze was blowing, though this high up, he couldn't taste the saltiness of it, and it just came through as a cool wind. He sat in one of his patio chairs and opened the file.

Brief biographies took up the first three pages. Michael Blum was a successful CPA with a company downtown. He had come from a good family in Los Angeles and his father had been an insurance salesman, his mother a stay-at-home mom. His father died of cardiac arrest at the age of fifty-eight. Michael was fifty-three. Stanton could imagine the tightening dread that must've been choking him as he approached the age of his father's death. He had no criminal history, other than a "failure to stop at the command of a law enforcement officer" charge.

Stanton had seen that charge frequently in the upper-middle-class when they had no other history to speak of. They'd run a stop sign, or violate some other traffic law, and then notice the police officer camped across the street and try to get away. Their interactions with police were so rare that even a ticket frightened them and they'd panic.

Nina Blum had come from a wealthy family, far wealthier than her husband. Her father had been the CEO of a telecommunications company. Nina had attended Vassar before moving to California to pursue a career in acting. Michael had married late: when he was forty-four and Nina was twenty-six. The biographies were simple summaries Sherman had written up. They didn't include some of the details Stanton would have pursued and written in, like how they had met.

Stanton flipped quickly through the autopsy and toxicology reports, scanned the ballistics report again to refresh his memory, and then got to the photos. Nina Blum, for all the terror and pain she had gone through, had been left mostly intact. The breasts and buttocks had not been mutilated—with the exception of about twenty bite marks—which was rare for a disorganized killer. Usually, long sessions of tearing and/or cutting were associated with this type of offense. Many times, they would eviscerate their victims or amputate limbs and breasts. But Nina's only real disfiguration was a small pinprick on her left arm where massive amounts of heroin had been injected before the sexual assault.

One thing that Stanton had noticed the first time he saw this photo was that Nina Blum had make-up on. It was possible she had gone to sleep with it, but there was little evidence of it on her pillow or clothing. So either she woke up in the middle of the night and put it on, or *he* had forced her to put it on.

The last eight photos were of Michael and the children. Stanton flipped through them until he came to the last photo: one of the boys' stamped hands.

"What're you looking at?"

Stanton was startled but didn't show it. He looked up to Emma's soft eyes and quickly closed the file, placing it on a side table.

"Nothing. Just an old file for work."

She sat down next to him. The ocean was less than a couple hundred feet away and they watched the setting sun as it glimmered off the water.

"Have you ever thought about giving it up, Jon?"

"Investigation? Why?"

"It wears on you. Not as much as being a detective, but it still wears on you. It seems like a lot of the kids you find are dead. Chasing corpses can't be very fulfilling."

"A lot of them are, but not all of them. Some of them are runaways. Some of them were kidnapped by relatives and taken out of state. There's some reward in that."

"You ever thought about teaching? I think it'd be fun for you to be in our psychology department. Or what about opening your therapy practice?"

Stanton shook his head. "I definitely wouldn't do that. All the studies suggest that one type of therapy isn't any better than another. Psychoanalysis doesn't work any better or worse than cognitive behavior therapy, which doesn't work better or worse than electroshock therapy. Progress is based solely on the skill of the individual therapist. That's not science, that's art. I'm not sure how good of an artist I would make."

"I think you'd be great at whatever you wanted to do. I just don't think this is it. You take things too personal."

"What do you mean?"

"Like when you're talking to someone new. You talk like them—you take on their speech patterns and vocabulary. I used to think you do it on purpose, to fit in, but I realized it's completely unconscious. You absorb things from the people around you. And if those things are nothing but death...I just don't think this line of work is for you anymore."

She reached over and held his hand. They watched the entire sunset without a word before going inside and lying together on the couch. They watched a movie before Emma kissed him goodnight and left.

He went back out on the balcony and opened the Blum file.

CHAPTER 5

Stanton woke up and got a slight thrill knowing it was Friday. Though Sundays were spent in church, on Saturdays he would turn off his cell phone and refuse to check emails. He would spend the entire day surfing and occasionally a massage would follow.

Next to him on the nightstand, the Blum file lay open, Mrs. Blum's lifeless, gray face staring up at him. He reached over and closed the file before rising and showering. After a breakfast of almond butter and mashed banana on toast, he headed out the door. He'd received the email he'd been waiting for from Anna Dopler: a list of the regulars at the swinger parties she attended.

She was shocked when he suggested that their sex life could have endangered her son, but after a few minutes she began to cry, admitting that sometimes she would host the parties at her home.

"Do you really think we caused this?"

"No," Stanton had said, "you didn't do anything to deserve this."

Stanton looked through the email as he got into his car. It was a list of eight couples that had attended the last party they had at their house. Anna insisted that everyone knew everyone else and that no strangers were there.

Stanton submitted the names directly from his iPhone to background review affiliates, and within minutes, received an email with their occupations, addresses, phone numbers, debt, collection matters, law suits, and criminal histories. He was most interested in the criminal histories.

A true sexual deviant couldn't control his urges once they began to manifest at puberty; occasionally even several years before or after. If intelligent, they would bring only minor offenses with them into adulthood, avoiding sex offenses as long as they could before being caught when their urges didn't allow them to stop, even when the risk was too great. If unintelligent, or careless, they would receive their first sex offenses as juveniles. Though the juvenile records were sealed, Stanton knew how to access them. Through the Office of Probation and Parole. He submitted a request on all eight couples. Those records would not normally be released to the public, but they made an exception for former detectives that went into PI work. A common practice in Southern California. It would be forty-eight hours before he received a reply.

As he pulled out of his parking stall, Stanton's phone rang. He recognized the first three digits: it was the District Attorney's Office.

"This is Jon."

"Yes, Mr. Stanton?"

"Yes."

"Please hold one moment for Assistant District Attorney Kathleen Ackerman."

The line clicked before a female voice came on.

"Jon Stanton. How have you been?"

"*Assistant* District Attorney. Congrats, Kathy. I always pegged you as switching to defense."

"What can I say? The benefits here are too good. So how you liking being a private citizen?"

"Can't complain."

"They really miss you over in Special Victims. They always tell me you're the one detective who didn't lose his temper even once under cross."

Images of two-week jury trials, the days wasted away in windowless courtrooms, filled his mind. He couldn't believe how much of his life he had thrown away inside courts.

"Who knows? Maybe a little spit-and-fire would've been

good for me."

Kathleen paused. "Jon, this is a little awkward for me, considering we haven't talked in a few years. But I have a favor to ask you."

"What?"

"Do you have time this afternoon to stop by my office? I'd like to ask you in person."

"That important, huh?"

"I think so."

"What time?"

"How about one?"

"That should be fine. I'll see you then."

"Okay, see you then."

Stanton hung up and got onto I-405, heading north to the first address on his list. He thought about Ackerman and her favor. She had asked him for favors before when he was a detective; usually minor things. But once Stanton thought she had crossed the line.

A young girl and her friend, both sixteen, had gone to a fraternity party at USD. When they got there, they realized they were the only two females at the entire party. They were plied with alcohol and when they were too drunk to run, the men pinned them to the couches in the living room and gang raped them for over three hours before throwing them out and making them drive home.

The girls crashed their car five minutes from the fraternity into a telephone pole. The responding officers noticed the blood stains on the front of their shorts and had the acumen to call the Special Victims detectives.

Seven of the eight men were charged with aggravated rape, forcible sodomy, assault, kidnapping, and several other misdemeanor charges. The eighth one was charged only with providing alcohol to a minor, punishable by a six-hundred-dollar fine.

Stanton was furious. The girls' statements said that all eight men engaged in the rape, and the SANE nurse—the forensic nurse that specializes in the collection of evidence in sexual assault cases—and the crime lab had submitted in their report that they collected eight separate semen samples between the two girls. The lead prosecutor on the case was Kathleen and Stanton stormed into her office, demanding to know why the last one had been given only a fine and a misdemeanor.

Kathleen had explained that some of the men confessed to the rape but stated that the last boy—Andrew Short—had not participated. That he had gone to bed during the rapes.

Stanton remembered when the boys had admitted that to him and Sherman during the investigation, but some of the men didn't recall that. In fact, several of them said that Andrew had participated.

When Stanton objected and demanded he be charged as well, Kathleen politely reminded him the final charging decision was hers. It wasn't until nine months later, when Andrew Short sexually assaulted a twelve-year-old girl in a mall bathroom, that the media—and Stanton—discovered that Andrew Short was the adopted son of Scott Kerr, chair of the California Democratic Party and one of then District Attorney Paul Kruger's biggest donors.

Stanton complained to IAD, and had one phone conversation with Kathleen. Paul Kruger wouldn't see him. He thought about going higher up with the complaint but the chief of police had stepped in and resolved the issue. Andrew Short was entering a plea deal with a six to life prison sentence. What more did Stanton want?

"What I want," he'd told the chief, "is for that little girl not to have gone through this."

The chief had sympathized but told him there was nothing he could do. Stanton never worked with Kathleen again and soon transferred out of Special Victims and back into homicide.

But Stanton never held a grudge. Grudges, he thought, only hurt the person having them, not the object of their hatred. He had forgiven her and moved on and they had worked several cases after that. Besides, she was probably ordered to do it and had little control over the situation. Paul Kruger was the one in charge, until being brought up on bribery charges by the FBI and resigning in disgrace.

Stanton rolled down his window and the warm air cleared his head. An accident had occurred up ahead and the traffic came to a dead stop. By the time he arrived at the address in Lakeside, it was nearly noon. He went to the door and knocked. Nobody was home. He left a note stating that he needed to speak with them. Whenever possible, he preferred showing up unannounced so people couldn't prepare themselves for questioning, but this would have to do.

He got into his car, flipped back around, and headed toward the District Attorney's Office.

The building was gray and at least twenty stories but appeared like something from a century ago. The current DA was a woman that had risen through the ranks with sheer grit, and one of the platforms she ran on was cost cutting and no frills. She had even taken out the water coolers; employees were expected to bring in their own bottles of water.

Stanton parked in a pay lot across the street and went in. He asked the security guard for Kathleen Ackerman and he said she was in Special Prosecutions on the fifth floor.

Special Prosecutions dealt with cases that had been flagged as potentially causing problems. In these cases the defendant or victim was typically related to a high-ranking police officer or one of the prosecutors or any politician. The cases would be handled with more care and discretion. Cases that received media attention were immediately transferred to Special Prosecutions also. For a prosecutor, the SP unit was the best place to be: you received the lightest caseload and the most media exposure.

Stanton stepped off the elevator and let the receptionist know he was there for Kathleen. When Stanton was led to the corner office with the plush leather furniture, he saw two men waiting for him with Kathleen sitting behind her desk.

One of the men was Danny Childs, the other he had never met.

"Jon," Kathleen said, "so glad you came. Please have a seat."

Stanton glanced at Childs but didn't say anything as he sat down. He had a feeling he knew what he was about to be put through.

"Jon, this is Kyle Bonnie. He's been informed that Philip Oster wants to make a confession and show us where the bodies are buried for several of his victims." She paused. "His daughter was one of them."

Stanton felt anger rising inside him. He watched Childs, who wasn't looking in his direction but out the window.

"Mr. Bonnie," Stanton said, "I'm very sorry for your loss. But I can't help you." Emma's comment the night before last had only strengthened his resolve.

"Detective, I want you to know something: I had lost hope of ever knowing what happened to my daughter. You haven't lost a child so you don't understand, but it's really important to find out what happened. Because you just keep thinking of the worst. Of how much she must've suffered. And then the worst part is this glimmer of hope that maybe they're still alive. That maybe they're chained up somewhere in some cabin and they're...and they're calling out for you.

"I'm in so much pain I can't sleep at night. I've been on anti-depressants now over a year, ever since Jill was taken from me. Her mother ran out on us when Jill was five so it's just been us two her entire life."

"I understand more than you know, Mr. Bonnie. And I am sorry. But I'm not a detective anymore and I have no desire to be again. It took me a long time to get to where I'm comfortable with that, and I can't go back." Stanton rose. "If you'll excuse me, I have to be elsewhere."

Stanton escaped into the hall before Childs got to him and grabbed his arm. Stanton pushed him away and got in his face.

"If you ever sandbag me like that again—"

"I'm sorry, Jon. We didn't know how else to get you here."

"How about treating me with respect. How about calling and asking to meet with a victim's father like we're actually friends."

"We are friends. And I'm sorry. I can see it was wrong now. I'm sorry. But this case has stuck with me. Of all people, you know what that feels like. You feel like you would do anythin' to make it go away. I had to try, Jon. We had to try. Kathleen's been workin' her ass off on this case. She would never admit it, she's too tough, but I know it's gotten under her skin too."

"This was the wrong way to do it, Danny. No matter how you did it, my answer still would've been no, but at least I could've still trusted you."

Stanton left and didn't look back as Danny called his name.

CHAPTER 6

Once in the parking lot, Stanton had to walk around to calm down. He kept a little rubber stress ball in his glove box, and he pulled it out, squeezing it as he paced around the lot once. As he headed back to his car, he saw a man approaching. It was Kyle Bonnie.

"That was wrong, Detective. I'm sorry, I didn't want to do it that way but they said you wouldn't show up any other way."

"It's all right, I'll live. And just call me Jon."

"Jon, I know you have kids. They told me you did and that you'd understand. But until you lose one of 'em, you can't understand. It feels like one of my limbs is missing and I keep thinking it's there. She'd sometimes come and crash with me for a while when she and her boyfriend would get into a fight. In the middle of the night I would hear her call my name. She had nightmares from a sexual assault when she was young. I'd go in and comfort her and she'd say, 'I'm glad you're here, Dad.' That's all she would say, but that would keep me going. Just that line. I sometimes get up in the middle of the night 'cause I think I hear her and I go to her room. But it's empty."

Bonnie grew emotional and tears began to pour. Stanton stood quietly to let him finish. When he did, Bonnie wiped his tears and pulled out a photo from his wallet. It was of a beautiful woman in her early twenties; blond hair and crystal-blue eyes.

"That's my Jill. She was gonna be a runway model but things didn't work out like that. I know you judge her for being in those movies, but she was young. She asked me if it was okay and I told her that she was an adult and I trusted her to make the right decision. Maybe if I had put up a fight…I don't know. I don't know."

"Mr. Bonnie, I—"

"I know. It's unfair of me to even ask. But I hope you understand why I had to ask. Thank you for your time, Jon."

Bonnie turned and walked away. Stanton watched as he walked in one direction and then realized he was going the wrong way. He turned and went toward a car that was parked at a meter on the street.

Stanton saw him get into the driver's seat, and put his head down on the steering wheel. He was there a long time before sitting up, and driving off.

Stanton walked into Young Hall on the UCLA campus. The drive had been clear and he listened to an album by INXS on the way up. Walking down the long corridor, looking at the fliers up on the walls advertising everything from roommates to laboratory assistant jobs, he felt relaxed. But every once in a while, his stomach knotted and he'd have to push the anxiety out of his mind and think about his boys or the beach or a pleasant book he'd read.

On the right-hand side of the corridor, he found the classroom he was looking for. It sloped downward to a podium and two massive chalkboards. He guessed there were just over twenty students in the classroom and he was surprised there were even that many. Emma only taught graduate-level courses in quantum theory and thermochemistry. Though it was nearly only a side project, she was revered as one of the top arson investigators in the world. However, she refused to consult on cases anymore. Now she just taught and researched in the laboratory. Calls from police departments and defense attorneys for help in arson cases were left unreturned.

Stanton stood in the back of the classroom and watched as Emma wrote an equation on the board.

"So the uncertainty principle tells us that both the position and the momentum cannot simultaneously be measured with complete precision. But we can measure the position of a moving free particle, creating an eigenstate of position with a wave function that is very—"

She froze when she saw Stanton. A quick smile and she continued.

Stanton sat down in one of the seats and listened. He had little knowledge of what she was speaking about. He had preferred his literature and art classes to science. Though psychology was the major draw, he had contemplated getting his doctorate in art history, but he wasn't sure what avenue he could have pursued with that.

When the class was over and Emma had spoken to a few of the students, Stanton rose and went down to meet her by the podium. She kissed him on the cheek and said, "Help me with my laptop."

"Your students love you."

"How can you tell?"

"I just can. The guy in the glasses and blue shirt looked like he might pass out talking to you, though. I think you've got an admirer."

Emma chuckled. "He's a good student. He's going to make a brilliant chemist one day."

They began walking up the steps and Emma reached down and held his hand. It was pleasant, but it had surprised him and he pulled back a little at first. He could tell she had noticed.

"There's a great sandwich place near here if you're hungry," she said.

"Sure."

Stanton watched the students as they walked across the lawn and hurried in between the buildings. They appeared so young; it was difficult for him to believe he had ever been that young. Or that he had thought he actually knew how the world worked at that age. It was fun to think how foolish your professors were and how much more you understood than they did. Learning that you really didn't know anything was a hard lesson. And once learned, it could never be unlearned.

Stanton loaded the laptop and Emma's bag into her backseat. He got in the passenger side as she returned a text and started the car. They pulled away and headed toward Sunset before following the road east toward a string of restaurants.

"Daniel Childs came to see me the other day," Stanton said.

"Really? What for?"

"An old case of mine that was unsolved. They have someone in custody that confessed to it."

"Did he have to come see you in person for that?"

Stanton was impressed by how perceptive she was. "No. The suspect wants to talk to me."

"Why?"

"I don't know."

"Well, you said no, right?"

"Of course."

"Good." She was silent a moment. "There's more, isn't there?"

"The father of one of the victims was at a meeting I got duped into going to."

"So what?"

"I don't know. Nothing I guess. Just the way he asked for help...I've never gotten used to how desperate victims' families can become."

"Jon, there's a whole police force out there that Danny can use. He doesn't need you. Not anymore. Let them take care of it. How many fathers of victims have you spoken to over the years? Dozens? Hundreds? You can't stop it. There will always be victims and there will always be families of victims. You can't help all of them."

"I know. That's why I told him no."

Behind the sandwich shop, Emma put the car in park. "You never just pop in to my classes. So what were you looking for? For me to tell you it's okay? That you should just do this one thing for them and that it's all right by me? Well it's not. I don't want you to do it. They've used you so many times and what do you have to show for it other than scars?"

"I told them no, Emma. There's no reason to get upset."

She took a deep breath. "I'm sorry. I just can't go through that again. What we went through with Stark…I just couldn't handle it again."

Stanton hadn't heard his name mentioned out loud in over a year and it made him uncomfortable to hear it now. "I think I'd like a vacation. Let's go on a cruise."

"Now you're talking," she said, getting out of the car. As they walked into the restaurant, she said, "Where do you want to go?"

"Europe. I've always wanted to see Athens. You ever been?"

"No, never."

After being seated near a window, they ordered and sipped their drinks quietly. Stanton could tell she was thinking about their trip, about the places they would visit and the food they would eat and the cultural landmarks they would see. He tried to think of it too, but his mind wouldn't let him. He saw a father sitting in his car, thinking about the death of his only child. Images like that would stick with him and he'd try to push them away, but never could.

"Oh my gosh," she said.

"What?"

"You're going to do it."

"Do what?"

"Don't BS me, Jon. I can see it in your face. You're going to meet with this psycho."

"Emma, I told them no. They won't contact me again about it."

"Let me ask you something; if you don't do this, are you going to regret it?"

"No, I won't regret it. He's already in custody so there won't be any more victims."

She nodded. "I'm asking you not to do it and I'm trusting that you won't."

"I don't know what the right thing to do is, but I won't go anywhere near it, I promise."

CHAPTER 7

Henry Grimes stood up in the courtroom and buttoned the top button on his suit before approaching the jury.

After a previous six-day trial where they broke for only thirty minutes for lunch every day, every inch of him felt exhausted. But he had no choice: the witness he needed was only available today. He had to go forward with the trial now.

He was a larger man, over three hundred and thirty pounds, and he had to wipe the sweat from his brow with the pocket square from his two-hundred-dollar suit. He looked down to the worn-out black shoes on his feet and wondered if the jury had noticed. Not that he really cared: all his clients were referrals now and there were better things to spend money on than clothes.

"When I was fourteen-years-old," he began, standing no more than five feet from the jurors, "my friend Emilio started slowly robbing a video game store. He would go in with a few other guys from our junior high school and pack up his coat with video games. The other guys would distract the cashier and they'd make off with six- or seven-hundred-bucks' worth of games. Then they'd go to a used game store down the block and sell them. Pure profit.

"Well one of the employees noticed how many games were missing after a month or so of this and she called the cops. The cops brought over a yearbook from our school, which was the closest one, and the cashier identified Emilio, two of the other guys, and my best friend, Josh. Josh had nothing to do with the thefts. He was a good Jesus-loving kid who went to church every

Sunday and wouldn't so much as have a drink of beer at a party. But he had the misfortune of looking like one of the boys that was stealing from this store with Emilio.

"So, the cops go and pick Josh up. They interrogate him, without his mother or father, for over ten hours. Sun up to sun down. They have him in a little room and two detectives are grilling him. They don't let him eat; they don't let him use the bathroom. In fact he wet his pants about four hours in 'cause he couldn't hold it anymore. But the detectives kept going because for some crazy reason, he wouldn't confess. He kept telling them he had no idea where the games were being stolen from or who was stealing them. But they don't believe him because an eyewitness saw him do it.

"Well after ten hours, the detectives are fed up. They've had hardened killers break after just a few hours and this punk kid is resisting every trick in the book. But Josh is breaking down too. He's scared and wants to go home. One of the detectives says, 'Look just confess, and we'll let you go. Nothing will happen.' Josh believes him and says, 'Okay, I did it. Can I go now?'

"Instead of getting to go home, he got handcuffs slapped on his wrist. He was charged with robbery, theft, burglary, and false information to a police officer. His mother had the wherewithal to hire a good attorney and the case was dismissed against him six months later when the actual boy was caught stealing something else and confessed to these crimes. But for six months, it ruined Josh's life.

"People at church looked at him different, friends stopped hanging out with him, his own mother didn't believe him when he said he didn't do it. Their relationship, I think, was never the same for the rest of his life. Cops make mistakes. We love to believe that our government is infallible but Josh's story is not unique. Things like that happen all the time."

Grimes walked from one side of the jury box to the other and planted himself.

"Now, this is a drug case, but the same principle applies: the cops made a mistake. You'll hear from the State's primary wit-

THE PORN STAR MURDERS

ness, what's known as a CI, a confidential informant. This man is the lowest of the low in the criminal world. He's a man who sells the lives of others to earn favor for himself. Much of the time, he sells out his own friends for no more than sixty dollars to support a drug habit that—"

"Objection, Your Honor, sidebar," the prosecutor bellowed.

Grimes looked to her. She was wearing a tight, red suit that accentuated her hourglass figure. Grimes looked her up and down and lingered a little too long on her well-defined calves.

"Mr. Grimes," the judge said, "care to join us?"

"Of course, Your Honor."

He walked up to the bench and leaned against it as the prosecutor waited for him. She didn't look at him but instead inclined close to the judge. Grimes figured they'd been sleeping together a while. His investigator had told him as much. After twenty years practicing criminal law, nothing surprised Grimes anymore.

"Your Honor," she began, "we had a clear order from the court established in limine that the CI's prior drug use and the number of cases he's cooperated with the government on are not to be introduced to the jury. I ask for an immediate mistrial."

"Judge, she just wants a mistrial 'cause she knows my witness is leaving the country for good the day after tomorrow and I may not be able to get him back. And what the order on the motion in limine stated is that I can't discuss specific instances of his drug use and specific instances of his cooperation with the government—which, all due respect, I still plan to appeal should I lose this trial. I'm speaking in generalities about things he's going to talk about anyway. Unless he plans to get up there and lie and say this is the first case he's flipped on, it's gotta come up that he's done this before."

"You're pushing it, Mr. Grimes," the judge said. "You may not agree with my rulings but they are my rulings. It was more prejudicial than probative. And you can fight it out with the Court of Appeals." He turned to the prosecutor. "Nice try, but

I'm not granting a mistrial. I'll just issue a curative instruction."

"Your Honor, I think—"

"That's enough. A curative instruction will be sufficient. Thank you both." As the attorneys walked away, the judge turned to the jury. "Ladies and gentlemen, you will disregard Mr. Grimes' last few statements. The informant's history and prior drug use or lack thereof is not pertinent here."

Grimes scoffed, loud enough for the jury to hear. The judge turned red but didn't say anything.

Finishing up his opening statement, Grimes sat down. The judge looked to the clock. It was past noon. Voir dire—jury selection—and opening statements had taken four and a half hours. He ordered an hour break for lunch. Grimes gathered up his files and stood as the bailiffs escorted out the jury. He watched them closely, hoping for one to smile at him or his client. Nothing.

Grimes walked out of the courtroom and heard the prosecutor stomping up from behind.

"What the hell was that bullshit?" she said as they began walking down the corridor to the exit.

"That ruling was crap and you know it."

"So appeal it."

"I will and I'm going to win and we're going to have another trial. Unless I win right now." He stared at her legs again. "We're still willing to take a misdemeanor any time."

"Guy's a drug trafficker. No way."

"Suit yourself. But this case is gonna take a long time. I've been known to keep things in appellate limbo for years."

"Up yours, Hank."

As she stormed away, Grimes stared at her ass until she was all the way outside the building. He waited a few moments and then followed her.

Just as with his suit, Grimes didn't care much about his car. It was an old Buick, dusty and beat up. What the hell? He didn't have anyone to impress. As he climbed in, he took out his Android and dialed his investigator.

"What's up, Hank?"

"Did you get the names of the jurors I sent you?"

"Yeah, man. I'm running 'em right now."

"This trial'll go until tomorrow but no later. I need 'em quick."

"I'll have 'em to you by tonight."

"Quick, Kris."

"All right, gimmie three hours. Did you hear about our boy?"

"What boy?"

"Oster, man. He sent a letter down."

"What's it say?"

"He says he got your message that Jon Stanton won't meet with him. He says to cancel any other meetings with the DA's Office."

Grimes shook his head. "That stupid son of a bitch. They're gonna fry him. This might be his only way out."

"I know, you're preaching to the choir. But he won't do it."

Grimes exhaled. "I'll handle it."

"Okay, cool. See ya."

Grimes hung up and dialed the number to the Special Prosecutions section. He was on hold for over two minutes before Kathleen Ackerman's voice came on the line.

"What do you need, Hank?"

"Philip Oster. It's a no go. You can cancel the meeting for next week."

"He's gonna want to hear what I have to offer."

"Yeah, I know. But he won't meet without Stanton."

"Jon's retired. I can't force him to do the meeting."

"Well Oster's got some sort of hard-on for him, so no Jon, no bodies."

She exhaled. "Off the record, is this legit?"

"Off the record, get Stanton there and find out your damn self."

"Don't be an asshole, Hank. You're already fat and no one likes a fat asshole."

"I'm happy to show you how this fat boy rolls in the bed. Any time, Kathy."

"I'll get Stanton there. Keep the meeting on your calendar."

"If you say so."

He hung up, a grin on his face. She's desperate, he thought. One of the victims' families must be well connected or wealthy. Even in this country, one could buy justice. Grimes called his investigator back.

"Keep the meeting on. Send Philip a letter telling him Jon Stanton will be there."

CHAPTER 8

Stanton sat in his car. It was a Wednesday, just after two, and the residential street he was parked in was empty; only a few housewives driving kids to or from lessons and school. He watched the home of the DeMarias.

Mario and Chloe DeMaria had been part of the swinger community for over twelve years. Since they had been married for only eight, that meant they were swingers while still dating. Stanton guessed they met at one of these parties. Each of them had a previous marriage under their belts.

They had attended the Dopler's last party.

Mario DeMaria had three sex offenses on his criminal history: sexual battery, harassment, and lewdness. All misdemeanors. It was the beginning of a career in sex crimes, or the end. However, the odds were that DeMaria was a sexual deviant whose urges grew more and more powerful by the day. It was extremely rare for a sex offender to suddenly stop and develop the ability to control his behavior. But Stanton had seen it once before.

Stanton's door suddenly opened and a woman stepped inside and sat down in the passenger seat. Stanton instinctively reached for where his firearm would have been if he were still with the force, and felt an emptiness that surprised him. He then noticed Kathleen's soft face with its large brown eyes and relaxed. She was holding a thick folder.

"How'd you find me here?" he asked.

"Your secretary. Don't be mad at her. A badge from the DA's Office can be pretty persuasive."

Stanton exhaled and looked back to the DeMaria house. "You know, I told my girlfriend that you guys wouldn't actually ask me about this again."

"I have to. I don't have a choice."

"Why not? It's just one case. You'll have dozens more just like it."

She shook her head. "Not like this, Jon. You saw what he did to Nina Blum. Imagine that over and over again. I understand that the women were adult film actresses and the public's not exactly sympathetic to the group. They barely cared about it when the story broke. But that's why I do care. These women come from abusive backgrounds. Almost every one has history of childhood rape and molestation. They get addicted to drugs, and they give up hope. The more films they make, the more strangers they have sex with, the more hope they lose. They're lost, and they don't have anybody fighting for them."

"You care about this that much, huh?"

"I do. And you're the only one that can help me."

Stanton was silent a few moments, staring out at the DeMaria house. "Have you ever heard of the Stanford Prison Experiments?"

"No."

"They were conducted by a psychologist at Stanford named Philip Zimbardo. He essentially took average undergraduate students and assigned them randomly as either guards or inmates in a make-shift prison he set up in a basement at Stanford. The experiment was supposed to test how people behave when their environment is altered. It was intended to be a two-week experiment. They had to shut it down after six days.

"Within six days, the guards were abusing the prisoners so badly that there were safety concerns. They were torturing them and the torture was getting worse and worse. And these weren't hardened criminals or war veterans. These were normal, middle-class kids. Zimbardo had assumed the role of warden. He wouldn't do much but inspect the guards. Later in his life he looked at photos from those six days and saw something unusual: he was walking with his chest puffed out and his hands behind his back. A posture he never had before or since. It's the posture of someone in power, of someone in control ensuring order. You can see the same posture in Nazis as they inspected the extermination camps.

"Zimbardo remembered that during the experiment he showed his girlfriend photos of some of the prisoners. They were wearing buckets on their heads and being hauled to the bathroom. They had been singing as the guards were yelling at them and abusing them. He told his girlfriend how interesting it was and she began to cry. She said she didn't even recognize him anymore.

"He was the administrator of the test, Kathy. And he didn't recognize evil after six days. Six days, that's all it took for good men to become evil. That's why power is so insidious. There're a lot of good cops in this city but it seems like the only ones moving up to the top are the wicked. They're corrupt and nepotistic and turn a blind eye to any wickedness they see. That's why I can't come back. I can't help you."

She nodded. "I understand. I'll show you one thing and then I'm going to leave and I promise I won't bother you about this again." She opened the folder. Stanton recognized it as the murder book from the Blum case, except there were some documents and photographs he hadn't seen before.

"What is that?" he asked.

"The Blum file. The real Blum file. After Sherman's house was raided, they found this in his closet. Looks like he'd always been fascinated with this case. There're photos and reports in here that he didn't put in the official murder book at the precinct."

Kathleen flipped through some of the pages until she came to a notes section. It was filled with Sherman's scribblings. At the very bottom of the page, one line jumped out to him: P. OSTER. PRIME SUSPECT.

"P. Oster," Kathleen said. She let it sink in. "Jon, he knew who the killer was. Somehow, with all this evidence he withheld from us, he figured it out and never told us. I don't know how many people Philip Oster has killed, but anyone he killed after this incident is on our heads. We had him, and one of our own let him walk."

CHAPTER 9

Natalie Heath stepped out of the restaurant as her boyfriend Dillon finished paying. She walked onto the sidewalk and glanced up to the moon. Hanging in a cloudless sky, it appeared majestic in its loneliness. She wondered if there were people in the world that still said prayers to the moon, like our ancestors had.

"Ready?" Dillon said.

"Yup." He pulled out a small joint from an Altoids tin in his pocket and lit it. They passed it around a few times before he carefully put out the tip and placed it back in the tin.

The sidewalk was clean and had no cracks. It wasn't something she was accustomed to and it was one of the reasons she loved coming to the rich neighborhoods. That, and the fact that there were no billboards. Nothing destroyed the beauty of a location like ugly, mind-polluting billboards and she was glad this portion of the city didn't allow any.

"When do you wanna tell your parents?" Dillon said.

"I'm flying out there in two months."

"I'd come but I don't think your dad likes me."

"He likes you," she said, wrapping her arm around his. "He just doesn't know what you're going to do. He thinks you should go to college and major in accounting or engineering. Something so that you have a good way of providing for me."

"I think you're doing just fine providing for yourself. You'll pretty much always make more than me 'cause of this," he said, reaching down between her legs.

She giggled and kissed him. The kiss was soft and wet and his hand began to stroke her. She bit his ear and whispered, "Let's go to the roof." She was looking at the apartment building across the street. She had always wanted to make love on the top of a roof in the moonlight.

Dillon nodded, his will subject to whatever she wanted. She took his hand and began to lead him across the street.

As they stepped into the road, a van door slid open. The van was parked next to them on the curb. A man in glasses and a hat jumped out, shoving a gun in Dillon's face. Natalie screamed as the man grabbed her by the waist and began to drag her away.

Dillon rushed at the man but he cocked the trigger. Dillon froze in his tracks. The man pulled Natalie, screaming and biting and kicking, into the van and slid the door closed. He got into the driver's seat, the gun still pointed at Dillon's head, and peeled away.

Dillon stood in shock. Then, in a rage, he began chasing the van. He sprinted two or three blocks, shouting at it. The van seemed to play with him, slowing down until he got near and then taking off again.

But eventually the two red lights began to fade into the darkness, and were gone. He stood by himself, panting in the road, his hands on his hips.

He pulled out his phone and dialed 9-1-1.

CHAPTER 10

On Sunday, Stanton arrived early to church. The local Mormon church, known as a ward, was four miles from his house, and around seventy people attended in his time slot. He went from 9:00 a.m. to noon and usually surfed afterward.

As a speaker rose to the podium and gave a talk about the life of Jesus Christ, Stanton stared at the floor. He had slept only three hours last night and his eyes felt puffy. They were red at the edges. He hadn't been forced to ponder Eli Sherman in a long time.

He remembered the little things Sherman would do that gave Stanton pause but that he never followed up on. Not until after Sherman's murders came to light.

Once, Stanton had walked into his house to pick him up. The door was open and Stanton assumed he was in the shower. He went to the cupboard to get a bowl of cereal when he heard noise coming from the basement. Peeking down from the top of the stairwell, Stanton saw a nude female strapped in chains from the ceiling. Her name was Ashley and she had been dating Sherman for over a year.

Sherman was nude in front of a table filled with whips and small batteries hooked to wires and gags and leather bindings. He walked to Ashley and proceeded to whip her until she started crying. Then he comforted her by rubbing ice over her body, and they proceeded to kiss. He unstrapped her and she began to tie him up.

Stanton felt the urge to run down but it was obviously consensual. Instead, he went outside and waited in the car. When

Sherman finally came out, Stanton asked him what he had been doing. He said he had been working on the basement.

Ashley and Sherman dated another four months. One day, she just stopped showing up, and Stanton asked where she was. Sherman told him they had broken up and she had moved back in with her parents in San Francisco. Looking back on it now, Stanton couldn't believe he didn't follow up on her. But the thought of a police officer, a sex-crimes and homicide detective no less, murdering her, didn't even enter Stanton's mind. How could it? Sherman had completely blinded him.

If Sherman really had found Oster and let him commit his crimes, how many girls were there? How many people did he kill after Sherman already knew who he was? Oster had three months of freedom after the Blums before being arrested on his drug charge. If he truly was a disorganized killer with no control of himself, like he and Sherman initially thought he was, he could have easily committed half a dozen other murders in that time.

Stanton looked up and realized people were filing out of sacrament. He had missed the entire hour. He took a deep breath and stood to go to a Sunday school class when he saw Emma walk in. He grinned as she kissed him on the cheek, and without a word they began walking to a different room for the Sunday lesson.

Emma wasn't Mormon, and actually was a hardened atheist. The fact that she occasionally came to church and never said anything discouraging to him about it made him respect her even more.

The next two hours went much like the first: in a haze, Stanton couldn't pay attention to anything that was being said. He thought only of the families who had no idea that their daughter's murderer had already been identified by the police but had been allowed to roam free. He thought of Sherman sitting alone in his basement, reading about Oster's exploits, and the thrill he got knowing he was letting it happen. That was, at the end of the day, probably Sherman's real motivation: a sense of power.

That's what Stanton's education told him. But his gut told him something different. It told him that some people were just born evil.

Albert Fish, cannibal and mass murderer of several young children, would get in trouble on purpose at two-years-old in order to be spanked. His masochism only increased with age until, in his teenage years, it turned to sadism. The line between masochism and sadism was thin, and Stanton knew ultimately they went hand in hand.

"You okay?" Emma whispered.

"Fine."

When church ended, they walked out to Stanton's car. She wrapped her arms around him, and they leaned against his car, watching people pull out of the parking lot.

"Something happened," she said. "I can tell."

Stanton was silent.

"Whatever it is, I think you should talk about it. Isn't that what you psychologists always say? To talk about your feelings."

"I was presented with something today that brought up emotions I wasn't prepared for."

"What was it?"

"Evidence that Eli knew who killed the Blums and over half a dozen other young women, but kept it to himself."

"Whoa."

"Yeah."

"Are you...I mean are you gonna be in trouble?"

"I don't think so. He stole evidence from the file. There was no way I could've known what he was doing. Still, this is my fault."

"Jon, this is not your fault."

"I should have seen him for what he was. I have a doctorate in psychology. I was a detective for years before I met Eli. How could I not see it? He was murdering girls when he wasn't with me and I had no idea."

"You've told me before that truly intelligent psychopaths

are undetectable until they're caught because they screw up. Not because someone figures it out."

"This is different. He was with me. We spent ten-hour days together in a car. We ate our meals together. He would come over and spend time with my family, play with my kids. They called him Uncle Eli. I should have seen it, and because I didn't, every crime he committed when he was with me is my fault."

She looked him in the eyes. "You can blame yourself all you want, Jon. But it won't change the facts. That's why I went into science rather than one of the humanities or social sciences. No matter what I feel, the composition of carbon dioxide is still CO_2. And there's no way to change it. The only thing that can be changed is how I feel about it. You can go around blaming yourself because you didn't see him for what he was, or you can take your own analysis to heart and realize that a pure psychopath can fool anyone."

Stanton shook his head. "I know that on a theoretical level, but it doesn't take the guilt away. It doesn't take away Kyle Bonnie's face begging for my help to find his daughter's body. Those are facts, like you said, and I can never change them."

"So what are you going to do about it?"

"I'm going to help them. I'm sorry, Emma. I know I promised you I wouldn't, but this is a game-changer. Eli hid evidence that would have sent us right to Oster's doorstep. I need to know how many more girls there are. How many he took while his name was on a file in Eli's house. That's the only way I can live with myself. I'm sorry, but it's the only way."

She nodded and pulled away. "I can't be around that right now, Jon."

"I know. But it's just one interview at the prison. It'll be over in a week."

"Okay. Call me in a week then."

"Emma, wait."

She walked to her car and got in. She stayed for a few more moments and Stanton hoped she was adjusting the CD player or her make-up...anything other than crying. He watched as she pulled away and left.

Stanton took out his phone and dialed her cell. She didn't answer.

It was dark by the time Stanton changed into a wetsuit and went out for a night surf. On this stretch of beach near Sunset Cliffs, groups of youths lived in hostels or shared small apartments with others to keep their bills low and not have to work. They spent their free time surfing and getting stoned. Stanton would bring them food from time to time and listen to their stories. One young girl named Ione had struck up a friendship with him.

Stanton guessed she was no more than sixteen but she was mature for her age and filled with compassion. He frequently saw her give away the food he brought her to others she thought needed it more. Blond with dreadlocks and tan skin from long days spent in the sun, she was strikingly beautiful and the looks she got from men two to three times her age made him uncomfortable.

A bonfire roared near the shore, and Stanton walked past, receiving a few stares. Emerging from the group, Ione ran up and threw her arms around him, kissing his cheek.

"What's up, Johnny?" she said.

"I didn't see you at Ocean Beach yesterday."

"No, I was too blitzed to go out. Me and Teddy was chillin' here. The breaks are sick tonight."

Stanton looked to the men around the fire. The stares he received accused him of wanting to steal something that was theirs. "My offer still stands, you know."

She laughed. "What that you'll help me get a job and put me up in a place? I got a place, Johnny. I got a job."

"What job?"

"I sell pot."

"That's not a job. And I'm not even saying a nine-to-five. Let's figure out what you like to do and then find a way for you to make money at it."

"I like getting stoned and surfing. If you can get me a job doing that, I'll take it."

Stanton grinned. Once, when he wasn't too much older than her, he had lived on a beach similar to this one. Sharing a two-bedroom apartment with nearly twenty people, living on one candy bar a day just so he could go out every morning on the waves. They were some of the fondest memories of his youth, even though he wasn't much more than a vagabond.

"You don't know men, Ione. You think these people are your friends, but they only want what they want. And it's never about you."

"Aw, are you worried 'bout me, Johnny? That's so cute." She leaned in and kissed his cheek. "But don't worry, I'm good. I been on my own since I was ten. After your set come up and chill for a bit."

"Okay."

Stanton walked away. He laid down a towel and placed his keys and cell phone on it. He looked back once and saw Ione cuddling up to a Hells Angels-looking guy and taking puffs off a joint. Stanton turned back to the ocean and walked into the cool sea.

Finishing his set nearly an hour later, Stanton lay down on the sand and stared at the night sky. The stars were so bright they rivaled the moon, and cloudy puffs of white looked like galaxies sprawled across the blackness. He thought of his boys and took out his phone to give them a call. Melissa, his ex, answered.

"Hi, Jon."

"Hey. How are you?"

"Good. What's going on?"

"I was hoping the boys were there."

"Matt's out and Jon Junior's asleep. It's past eleven here."

"I know. I just felt like talking to them right now." He paused.

"How is everything?"

"Good, fine. How are you? I heard your little agency is doing well."

"It is. I'm starting to have to turn away clients."

"I always knew you'd be good at that. Better dealing with clients I bet than dealing with criminals." She was silent a moment and Stanton could hear her step into a different room. "The boys want to come out. They miss the ocean."

"It's in their blood. I don't think I could live without the ocean."

"You don't have to tell me. I remember how depressed you would get when you weren't near it. You'd curl up inside yourself and wouldn't let anybody else in." She was silent a moment. "But that's good. At least you know the cure for your dark places. Most people never find out."

"Yeah." He sat up and dug his toes into the sand. He glanced over to the bonfire and saw some of the young men sprinting and leaping over it, squealing from the pain of having their legs and bottoms burned. "Tell the boys I miss them."

"I will. Take care of yourself, Jon."

"Thanks."

Stanton hung up. When he went to put the phone down, he saw he had a text:

call me -Danny

He dialed Childs' number. He picked up on the first ring.

"Where you been?" Childs said. "I've been callin' all day."

"I don't work on Sundays, Danny."

"Oh, right. So, can you talk?"

"Let's talk tomorrow morning."

"Okay. But I just wanted to say one quick thing: I had no idea about what Kathy told you on Friday. If I did, I would've been straight with you."

"I didn't figure you did."

"So we cool?"

"Yeah, we're cool."

"Good. That's some crazy shit, though."

"I know." He paused. "I'm gonna do it, Danny. I'm gonna meet with Oster."

"Really? Why?"

"I think there're more vics, and I think we could've had this guy before he got ahold of them if Sherman hadn't buried the evidence."

"Yeah, maybe. I wouldn't beat yourself up about it, though. Kathy said it was just a name in a file. Maybe Oster called in and Sherman just wrote his name down or something."

"I don't think so. I think Eli knew it was him but didn't tell anybody. It doesn't matter now. I'm going to meet with him— but that's all I'm going to do."

"Cool with me, brother. But we talked enough on your holy day. I'll catch you tomorrow."

"All right."

Stanton hung up. He watched the waves in the moonlight a while before gathering his things and walking back to his car. As he strode past the bonfire he saw Ione making out with two men. He stopped and walked over.

"I'm leaving, Ione. I'll see you later."

She pushed one of the men off her as the other continued to kiss her neck. "All right, Johnny. See you when I see you."

"Yeah." Stanton stood there, staring at them. He couldn't bring himself to turn away. One of the men noticed.

"You want in?" the man said. "Fifty bucks."

Stanton bit the inside of his cheek. "I'll give you each a hundred if you leave the beach right now."

The men looked to each other. "You got yourself a deal."

Stanton gave them the money as Ione watched on. When they were gone, she came over to him. "You know I'll just hook up with some other guys tomorrow night."

"Yeah, but you won't be hooking up with those two tonight."

She shook her head. "My knight in shining armor." She kissed him again and then sat back down near the fire, taking a joint out of someone's hand. Stanton watched her a while before getting into his car, and driving away.

CHAPTER 11

The Northern Precinct hadn't changed since Stanton had been there last. It was busy and crowded and, near the holding cells, stunk of humans packed tightly in closed spaces. Two uniformed officers staffed the reception desk and Stanton had to show them identification before they called Childs down.

"Johnny," Childs said, walking out in a tight, polyester muscle shirt, "you ever think you'd be back here?"

"I hoped not," Stanton said, shaking hands.

"Well come on back, we got an office ready for you."

Stanton followed him to the back offices. A small one with no nameplate on the door was open, filled with a desk, a chair, some files, and an old computer. No windows and no decorations.

"It ain't the Ritz, but I figured you wouldn't be here much anyway."

"It's fine, Danny."

"I know you like a separate workspace."

"The only way you can actually stop working is if you have a single place where you do it that you can leave."

"Now how come I don't think you ever stuck to that rule?"

Before Stanton could answer there was a ruckus up front. He looked to see a man in an Armani suit and a trimmed beard walk into the precinct. He hauled another man in cuffs who was screaming profanities. Stanton recognized the first man as Detective Stephen Gunn.

The last time Stanton had seen Gunn, he'd had to pull his firearm on him to keep him from hurting a woman that didn't deserve to be hurt. Gunn's last words to him had been, "Watch your back."

Stanton didn't want to greet him, but seemingly reading his thoughts, Gunn looked up at him and grinned. He got an officer to grab the suspect he was with and walked over.

"Jon Stanton," Gunn said, loud enough for all the precinct to hear. "Don't tell me you're back."

"How are you, Stephen?"

Gunn stood in front of him, a large, dopey grin on his face. His hands were behind his back but Stanton could see the tension in his face.

"You tell him, Danny?"

"Tell him what?"

"That we're gonna be working together."

Childs looked from Gunn to Stanton. "Is that a problem? You two were partners a while."

"I work alone, Danny," Stanton said.

"I know. I just want Gunn to have your back. Four eyes are better than two. He'll stay outta your way but I think it'd be good to have a badge with you."

Stanton looked to Gunn who nodded and said, "Fine with me."

As much as Stanton didn't want Gunn anywhere near him, it was always better to have a detective with you than not. Even if it was just to cut through the security measures at a prison. It wouldn't matter anyway: Stanton was just going to do the interview and then never come back here again.

"Well," Childs said, "I'll leave you two to it. Let me know if there's anything you need, Jon."

Gunn stayed, staring at Stanton. He took a step forward and said, "I been thinkin' 'bout you, Jon. Just the other day I wondered what it was you were up to in that big nice office of yours. Bet you think you're pretty hot shit, huh?"

"I couldn't let you hurt her. You're a cop."

"You know what that whore did? She went to IAD. She was tryin' to get into witness protection and the stupid bitch didn't realize IAD didn't have any witness protection. Even if they did, they wouldn't spend the dime on a whore drug addict." He shrugged and smiled. "Nothing came of it, though. She got busted on some drug charge and had bigger things to worry about than ratting me out. Let me ask you somethin', Jon: you really think I woulda killed her?"

"Yes."

"Then you don't know shit. I was just trying to scare her. And you pulled your piece on your own fucking partner." Gunn slapped his shoulder and began to walk away. "Probably won't find much love in this precinct, Johnny. You may want to work from home."

Stanton exhaled and turned to his small office. He shut the door behind him.

The chair was uncomfortable, and without windows, Stanton had the out-of-body sensation of not knowing whether it was day or night. He sat quietly in the chair and let his mind adjust. Then he opened one of the murder books that had been placed on his desk.

There were three books: Danielle Evans', Jenny Rivera's, and Nina Blum's. Even though Oster had confessed to six murders total, only three of the cases had bodies and had been confirmed as homicides. The others, including Jill Bonnie's, were technically Missing Persons' cases, and Stanton would have to get the files from them directly.

The murder books in a modern police precinct were now electronic, downloaded directly to a detective's iPad. Stanton appreciated that Danny had given him the hard files. He liked to feel the paper in his hands and physically flip through them.

Stanton had seen several people, on airplanes or at restaurants, attempt to flip pages in actual magazines as if they were on iPads or their phones. It was an evolutionary coping mechanism. Our brains adapt remarkably fast and if we read frequently on an electronic device and then attempt to read on paper, it will feel odd and out of place. Stanton thought we were slowly becoming a society completely reliant on technology.

Technology had its place, but he knew in-person interaction was declining in a way no civilization had ever seen. People could communicate with whomever they wanted now at any time. It was much more convenient than actually going outside and having face-to-face meetings. More and more, Stanton saw the art of body language and persuasion dimming in the younger generations. They were being raised a generation hooked to computers, adrift at sea when they had to interact with a live person.

Stanton remembered a study in which college students were asked to analyze the information a newscaster from CNN was relaying. One group was asked to analyze the news feed without the news crawl at the bottom of the screen. The other group had the crawl. The group without the news crawl scored upwards of twenty percent higher on critical analysis and memory of what the newscaster was reporting. Distraction prevented absorption. Seeing kids glued to their cell phones every waking moment, Stanton knew their absorption of their environments was declining, creating a society of the ill-informed who had trouble interacting with one another. Not the best recipe for a democracy.

Stanton pushed these thoughts out of his mind, and opened the murder book for Danielle Evans.

CHAPTER 12

Danielle Evans and Nina Blum could have been sisters. Stanton stared at the photo on the inside jacket of the file a long time, absorbing every curve and dimple and strand of hair. She was five foot three with blue eyes and silky blond hair—almost platinum—that came down to her shoulders.

The medical examiner's reports were next. Stanton read the autopsy first. It included photos too, but the image of the beautiful young girl with the silky hair was replaced by one of her nude, the Y incision going from collar bone to pelvis. Her face had been peeled off to examine trauma to the skull. The ME concluded the same thing he had concluded in Nina Blum's death: death by overdose of opiates. A small needle mark was found in her left arm. No mutilation to the body had occurred and the ME had concluded that the trauma suffered to the skull was a result of postmortem relocation of the body and had not occurred while she was still alive. The pools of blood in the room she had been found in had come from her husband and teenage son.

Stanton flipped through until he found the toxicology report. Her blood was negative for alcohol but positive for fluoxetine—the base of the anti-depressant Prozac—and massive quantities of an opiate the lab had identified as diacetylmorphine, better known as China White heroin. The lab was never great at determining the purity of a drug once it entered the bloodstream, but their estimation was that the heroin had a purity of ninety-three percent. The purity of most street heroin was in the sixty percent range. That meant that whoever had shot Danielle Evans and Nina Blum full of drugs to the point their hearts had stopped was a player in the drug game. Either a manufacturer himself or a distributor with a direct line to the manufacturer. The majority of people, no matter how much money they had, could not get heroin this pure. The involvement of a manufacturer or someone with a direct line fit Oster since he had a long record with drugs.

Stanton pushed aside the toxicology and began reading her bio.

Danielle was originally from Blue Ridge, Texas. He googled the town and found out it had less than a thousand residents.

She moved out to Los Angeles when she was seventeen-years-old and then moved to San Diego. Like most young girls that move to LA from small towns, she had probably been an aspiring actress. When the realities of the industry hit and she realized she was either going to have to wait tables or work a cash register, she turned to pornography.

Pornographers in Los Angeles were unlike those anywhere else in the country. A pornographer in the Midwest would have to hide his profession and be extremely careful of how he acquired his girls for fear of arrest and prosecution. Though pornography itself was protected under the First Amendment by the Supreme Court, cities and states had found ways to circumvent the laws and obtain convictions. Primarily by forcing pornographers to obtain a plethora of licenses, go through physical exams and STD testing, be in properly zoned areas for sexually oriented businesses, and in some small towns in the south, post on a public website that they were pornographers, a tactic meant to shame them away from their profession.

In Southern California they were rock stars. And many porn actors and actresses were linked to major and upcoming bands in the LA and San Diego music scenes. Musicians had found connections to porn gave their images a certain recklessness they tried to cultivate.

Stanton noticed that a report he routinely gathered was not in the murder book: a psychological profile. Few detectives went through the trouble of gathering one, but to Stanton, there was no piece of information more important when working a homicide involving a suspected psychopath. The victim's traits were just as important as the suspect's. Something about her and her specifically had drawn him, and Stanton needed to know what it was.

He flipped through the rest of the reports, hoping for the name of the psychiatrist that prescribed her the Prozac. There was none. He then looked over the forty plus photos of the crime scene—her bedroom in a condo uptown—hoping for a glimpse of the amber pill bottle. That wasn't in there either.

He got onto his computer and instantly felt uncomfortable on a PC, having switched to Mac after buying an iPad. It added to the discomfort he was feeling being back in a building full of cops.

Stanton googled Danielle's home address and then searched for psychiatrists within a fifteen-mile radius. There were six. With every prostitute and pornography star, he always assumed there had been some sort of sexual trauma. Whether that was early childhood molestation, or rape as the girls grew older and began spending more time around boys. The trauma is what triggered their desire to dominate sexuality rather than be a participant. For them, it was a type of self-medication, just as alcohol was to someone with chronic depression and anxiety.

Because of the sexual trauma, these women shunned male therapists and instead sought out females. Particularly older females that wouldn't be seen as competition and chip at their insecurity. Of the six psychiatrists, four were male. Of the two women left, one was in her thirties and the other was in her fifties. He called the latter.

"Dr. Grey's office, how may I help you?"

"Yes, I'd like to speak to Dr. Grey please."

"And what is this regarding?"

"A former patient of hers, Danielle Evans." There was silence on the other line. "I'm a det—I'm working with the detectives handling the investigation of her homicide and just have a few questions."

"Okay, hang on. I'll put you through."

The line went silent and a jazz song came on. Stanton counted thirty seconds before a female voice said, "This is Dr. Amanda Grey. How can I help you?"

"Hi, Doctor, my name is Jonathan Stanton. I'm here at the Northern Precinct with the San Diego Police Department. I've been brought in as a consultant on a homicide investigation for one of your former patients, Danielle Maria Evans."

"Um hm."

Stanton had to suppress a grin. If he had asked for confirmation that she was a patient first, Dr. Grey would've said it was protected information and not revealed anything. "Well I was just wondering if I could have some information."

Stanton cleared his throat. This was the most difficult part. Almost every psychiatrist he had ever given the pitch to had ranted about doctor-patient privilege and refused to hand anything over. It took some work to get them to change their minds.

"What type of information?"

"Preferably your session notes."

She was silent a moment. "Are you serious? What makes you think I would possibly hand those over?"

"She's passed away, Doctor."

"I don't care. Doctor-patient privilege survives death."

"I know. But it's waiveable in certain circumstances."

"And this isn't one of them."

Stanton paused a moment. "Dr. Grey, if Danielle had told you she was going to go out and stab somebody, you would have been ethically bound to report that to the police. This is no different. The man that killed her has killed several other women and if he's not convicted and put away, he'll continue to do it. This is a serious threat to public safety; same as if Danielle had made it herself."

"Sorry, you're not getting them."

"Then I'm afraid I'll have to get a court order."

"Yeah, you do tha—"

"After I call the media." A long silence on the other line. "You know a judge is going to give them to me. And once it's reported in the media, all your clients and all your potential clients will see that you handed over a patient's most intimate information to the police. It won't matter that you were forced to."

Stanton waited a beat but she didn't respond.

"Dr. Grey, if she were alive, do you think Danielle would want you to give me the notes to help me catch this person or not?"

Another silence before she said, "Fine. I'll give them to you and only you and I expect them to be returned to me as soon as you've gone through them."

"Of course."

"I'm not emailing them. Have someone come to my office and pick them up. Someone with police credentials I can call and check on. I also want something in writing stating that you are forcing me to hand over the notes under threat of obtaining a court order. You need to get that to me before you pick up the notes."

"I will. And thank you."

She hung up without saying goodbye and Stanton placed the phone down. He stretched his neck and leaned forward over the desk, digging into the rest of the file.

CHAPTER 13

It was six in the evening by the time Stanton had read the Evans and Rivera murder books twice and gone through Nina Blums' once more. He also spent a lot of time online, researching all of their social media postings before their deaths. His stomach growled and he realized he hadn't eaten or drunk anything since this morning.

"You still here?"

Stanton looked up and saw Childs at the door, his jacket in his hands and his car keys out. "Yeah. I'm done, though."

"Interview's ready for next Wednesday with Oster. Gunn and Ackerman are gonna be there with you. I think I might send down a security detail too."

"They'll have guards there," Stanton said, closing the murder books and turning off his computer.

"I want some of our people there." He paused. "So, you still into this Jesus freak stuff?"

Stanton grinned. "Yes, Danny. But I'd be happy to come out drinking with you."

Coochies alternated between being a cop bar and a surfer hangout. The police element grew stronger every year but the surfers didn't leave. There was something in the irony of hanging out with cops while they had bags of weed in their pockets that seemed to excite them.

Stanton sat down in the booth. He was surrounded by over a dozen officers taking up three booths and a table. The alcohol began to flow and he ordered a Sprite. Most of the officers there knew him and didn't give it a second thought, but a few of the rookies he hadn't met before asked him if he wanted anything more manly to drink.

"No thank you," he would say politely.

One officer was asking him about Eli Sherman and what it was like working with him when Stephen Gunn walked through the door. The officers hollered at him and another round was ordered. Gunn had always had the ability to make a crowd love him.

"Jon," he said, "can I talk to you outside in private a sec?"

"Sure."

The sun was still setting and Coochies was close enough to the beach that Stanton could see the orange reflections of light off the water. He was paying attention to that when Gunn's fist crashed into his gut.

Caught off guard, Stanton crumbled; he was down on one knee, unable to breathe, holding his hand to his stomach.

"That's for pulling a piece on me. And the next time you think you can—"

Stanton swung upward, connecting with Gunn's jaw and sending him reeling back. Shocked at the aggression, Gunn stood there and spit a glob of blood onto the pavement.

He rushed at Stanton and tackled him at the waist. He was on top of him, striking his face with blow after blow. Stanton snaked his hands up to Gunn's eyes. He gave one quick jab with his thumbs. It caused a sudden rush of pain in Gunn and he screamed as Stanton used the opportunity to spin him off.

Stanton was now the one on top, and he began pounding on him with fists and elbows. He wasn't as strong as Gunn but he was much faster and Gunn couldn't stop all his blows.

"All right!" Gunn yelled. He grabbed Stanton by the lapels of his jacket and flung him off.

Stanton lay on the pavement, out of breath and bleeding from his mouth. Gunn sat up, nursing a bloody nose.

"What the fuck are you doing here, Jon?"

"I don't know."

THE PORN STAR MURDERS

"You're not a cop anymore. Nobody wants you to be a cop. Except that sick fuck in prison."

He nodded as he pulled himself up. "I know."

"Then quit. Let the real cops handle this."

"He won't talk to you guys."

"So what?" Gunn said, wiping the blood off his face with the sleeve of his shirt. "The girls are already dead and that piece a shit'll be behind bars until he's seventy. Who gives a shit if he confesses?"

"The girls' parents do. They don't have a body. I keep thinking about their birthdays. There's no cemetery for them to visit on their birthdays."

Gunn stood up. "Little Johnny Jesus Freak. Always tryin' to help old ladies across the road." He began to walk back to the bar. "Just stay the fuck outta my way."

CHAPTER 14

The next day, Stanton went surfing and then spoke to his sons on the phone for twenty minutes each. It was a habit he'd developed: each of his sons got the same amount of time. Occasionally, they would want to get off but Stanton would bring up another subject they were interested in and just let them talk. He wanted both of them to feel like they were the most important things in the world to him.

He longed to just fly out there and pick them up and bring them home to San Diego where they were born. But that wasn't possible. His mother had become a devout atheist and the thought of Stanton taking them to church—a Mormon church no less—every week filled her with anxiety. It was a battle just to get them to come out for a few weeks during the summer and winter.

He called Emma and she finally answered. They spoke briefly and Stanton asked her to come over.

"Not until you're done with all this," she said.

He wasn't sure why she thought he could just ignore this case and go on like nothing was different. Stanton helped whomever he could. He had once helped a man in his church he barely knew remove a tree from his yard. It took all of a Saturday to do. Emma had made plans for them and was furious. She told him helping people leads to your own suffering and that it's better to just look out for yourself.

"What do you even get out of it?" she asked him once when they were relaxing on the beach.

"Nothing. If you expect anything, even just feeling better,

you'll be disappointed. You can't expect anything from helping others."

She shook her head. "I think reality is going to beat that out of you one day, Jon."

Stanton showered and headed out the door after breakfast.

He thought about Anna Dopler and her missing son. He'd tried to refer the case out to another investigator but Anna insisted she didn't want that. She would wait until he was done doing whatever was taking up so much of his time.

Stanton drove down to Central Precinct and the Missing Persons Division. A detective by the name of Crowley was sitting in a cubicle with a stack of files covering his desk.

"Detective Crowley," he said, coming up behind him. "I'm Jon Stanton."

"They're right here," Crowley said without looking up from his computer. He had pointed to three files on the edge of his desk.

Stanton picked them up and read the names: Jill Bonnie, Ashley Low, and Monique Isham. He walked out of Central and sat in his car to quickly flip through them. All the girls had blond hair and blue eyes. In Jill Bonnie's file, a note in the description stated that she'd had her breasts augmented. So had Danielle Evans and Jenny Rivera. Stanton had seen corpses of girls that had gone through breast augmentation excavated. It was disturbing to see the skeletons with two plastic blobs on their chests that didn't decompose.

None of the files mentioned anything about the girls working in the adult film industry. However, the address was listed in Jill Bonnie's file for her father's office. Stanton turned the ignition and began to drive there.

The office was in American Plaza and Stanton had to park underground. He found a spot near the elevators and watched as two men in suits walked in with a girl in a miniskirt. One of the men stared at her legs as he opened the door for her and watched her pass.

Inside, Stanton took the elevators to the fourth floor. Hilder and Gilchrest, Kyle Bonnie's accounting firm, took up half the floor. It was a modern space with glass walls and art deco up behind the receptionist's desk.

"Can I help you?"

"Yeah," Stanton said, "I'm here to see Kyle Bonnie."

"He's in a meeting right now. Would you like to wait?"

Stanton checked his watch. "Would you mind telling him Jon Stanton is here? I have an appointment in about forty-five minutes."

"I guess," she said, sighing. She got up and walked into a conference room down the hall. In less than ten seconds, Kyle Bonnie was out and greeting Stanton.

"Detective, I was going to call you. Lieutenant Childs had someone call and tell me you were doing the interview."

"Can we talk somewhere private?"

"Oh, yeah. Come on back to my office."

As they walked by the conference room, Stanton saw a table littered with bagels and coffee and soda. Every seat was taken and the men and women looked impatient.

"Sorry to interrupt," he said.

"Screw them," Kyle said. "It's a company we're doing some work for. They come in here every six months and bitch about their bill. Makes them feel important."

The same style art as the waiting area's decorated the office, which had windows looking down on the street below. Stanton sat across from Kyle. He took out his iPhone and opened a note-taking app.

"So what can I do for you, Detective?"

"I'm not a detective anymore, Mr. Bonnie. Just call me Jon. I'd like to talk about something that might be uncomfortable for you but that I think is going to help me in this interview."

"Okay, shoot."

"How did your daughter get into the adult film business?"

Kyle exhaled. He stood up and shut the door before sitting

back down. "She made her first movie when she was eighteen. It was actually her high-school graduation. She was drunk and a couple of guys took advantage of that and they posted it all over the internet and started charging for it." He smirked. "Jill didn't take crap from anyone, though. She hired a lawyer and got all their profits. Every last cent. After that, she started looking for roles. Once she saw how easy the money was. She made more than me the first year and I have eight years of higher education."

"How many films was she in?"

"I don't know. I didn't keep count of that kinda stuff. She did it for four years, though, and she was co-owner of a production company so it had to have been a lot. I guess."

"Did she have a boyfriend?"

"Yeah, some actor she met on one of the sets. Um, Randy B. Dicks. I'm guessing that's not his real name. I met him once and he was a real asshole."

"Did she ever complain to you about anybody stalking her? Maybe just weird phone calls or the same person showing up at different places?"

"She did tell me once she was going to bed late after a party and she glanced out her window and Randy was there. He didn't say anything. He was just standing by a tree, staring up into her window."

"Do you know where I can find Randy?"

"He works on the same lot Jill did for a while. She got bigger than him and ended up leaving. I think he's been pretty pissed about it ever since. It's over in Hillcrest. I think it's called Galico Productions."

"You seem to know a lot about their relationship."

"There's nothing wrong with a father being involved in his daughter's life."

Stanton wrote it down and paused a moment longer than necessary before saying, "Where were you when she was kidnapped?"

Kyle stared at him a moment before his face flushed with

71

anger. "Are you fucking kidding me! You think I had something to do with it?"

"Not at all," he said calmly. "I'm just establishing where everybody was that knew her."

"I'm not stupid, Detective. How could you even think I could do anything to my little girl?"

"That's not what I'm saying, Kyle. I'm just—"

"I know what you're doing. But that sick fuck rotting in a cell confessed to my little girl's murder. Now do your job and go interview him and find out where her body is so I can bury my girl."

Stanton rose. "Thank you for your time."

As he walked out of the office, he made an additional note: CHECK KYLE BONNIE'S BACKGROUND.

CHAPTER 15

Stanton stopped at a roach-coach for lunch. It was nothing more than an RV with a sign for hot dogs on the side but he recognized it from his days on the force. The hot dogs were smothered in cheese and chili and the bun was stuffed with French fries before gravy was poured on top. He ordered one and a Diet Coke and sat down at a bench to eat.

He watched the traffic pass, the faces of the drivers. Some were angry, some were melancholy, few were joyful. He suddenly felt claustrophobic and had the epiphany that he had escaped something awful but hadn't realized how awful it was at the time.

He ate half the hot dog and wrapped the rest up in its wrapper. He threw it at a garbage can and missed and had to pick it up and toss it in before he took out his phone and called Emma.

"Hey," she said.

"Hey. How was class?"

"Good. You were right about that kid. He asked me out on a date today. He wanted me to come to his frat party."

"What did you say?"

"Jon, come on."

He grinned. "Well I don't know, maybe you like younger men?"

"No, I like my men old and grumpy." Stanton heard some papers shuffling. "What's going on?"

"Nothing. I just called to tell you the interview's in a couple of days. After that, I'm done and everything will get back to normal."

She paused. "I hope that's true."

"I'm telling you it is."

"I know, but sometimes you say things before you have all the information."

"I'd like to see you tonight."

She exhaled. "I miss you too. This punishment's been harder on me than on you I think. But I don't want anything else to do with the police world, Jon. It isn't a place I want to go. After my father's death I spent years trying to help the police find the person that actually committed the crime my father was executed for. I saw what power did to people, how it blinded them. I can't deal with that anymore. That part of my life's closed. It should be closed for you too. You've done enough for them. You don't need to do any more."

He hesitated. "It's not for them. I'd like to have dinner with you tonight. I think I should tell you something."

"What?"

"I'll tell you in person. Will you have dinner with me?"

"Yes, yes, of course I'll have dinner."

"Okay, I'll text you where to meet me."

"All right. I can't get outta here before seven, though."

"That's fine. I'll see you tonight."

"See you then."

Stanton hung up and walked back to his car. He pulled away and headed toward Hillcrest.

Stanton knew Hillcrest well. The streets were lined with storefronts and colorful awnings as if they were pulled from a painting of America in the early twentieth century. Boutiques, salons, coffee shops, and yoga studios dominated over large corporate chain restaurants and the people were friendly.

It was known as the gay and lesbian district. Many homosexuals moved here in the late seventies after housing discrimination precluded them from La Jolla and Mission Beach and some of the other nicer areas. But they made it their own and it was refreshing to be in a place that had such a youthful energy.

Galico Productions was in a warehouse surrounded by empty lots that were being developed. Stanton parked in front and took out a digital recorder from his glove box. He turned it on and put it in his pocket. Because he wasn't law enforcement anymore, he could record at will without the other party knowing and the recording would still be admissible in court.

He stepped out of the car as several women were leaving. They wore sweats and sneakers but their make-up was smeared and their hair appeared as if it had been immaculately manicured and then messed up purposely. He walked past them and smiled. They didn't smile back.

The front area had a receptionist's desk and a few chairs. A monitor showed the back of the warehouse.

A young woman with fake breasts and a revealing outfit came out. She noticed him and said, "Can I help you?"

"Yes, I was told Randall Jackson would be working today."

"He is. Are you a friend of his?"

"No, my name's Jon Stanton. I'm working with the San Diego Police. I'm investigating the death of Jill Bonnie."

The girl saddened. "I knew Jill. I really liked her. A lot of people in this business are fake, you know? But she was real. She would always help out anyone that needed it. I heard that guy in prison confessed to killing her."

"He did."

She nodded. "I'll go get him. Hold on a sec."

Stanton sat in one of the chairs and noticed the magazines that were on the coffee table in front of him. All pornographic, both hetero and homosexual. Buried underneath them was what looked like child pornography. Stanton pulled the magazine out. It was called *Lolitas in the Valley*. Though the girls appeared to be in their early teens, Stanton could see the photos had been doctored to give that effect.

Most pedophiles were like drug addicts, scouring around for the next hit without the consequences bothering them. That's why the FBI or SVU units of any police department in any city in the world could set up a fake child pornography website and make hundreds of arrests in a short period. But a few were able to control their urges long enough to ensure they wouldn't get caught. Magazines like this were made for them: the photographers would take eighteen-year-olds and doctor the photos to make them appear much younger.

For some reason, they never doctored the feet and ankles. You could always tell the photos had been manipulated because the skin would appear smooth everywhere but there. Stanton put the magazine back on the pile and leaned back in the chair. Fake moans echoed throughout the space.

The place had a dark energy that put Stanton on edge. Though he believed in a Satan, Satan didn't need to be more than a feeling, a darkness that would inhabit certain people and places. He had seen it over and over again in his work. A drug addict begins with a single hit, which invites that dark energy into his life. It begins to consume him and pretty soon that's all there is. Stanton had spoken with hundreds of drug addicts in his work, and the way they looked, the words they said, even their voices, over time, were not theirs. It was as if they were being controlled by something external. Darkness penetrated and surrounded them.

He got that same feeling in this studio.

The door flung open as a man walked out. His head was buzzed and he was tall. With his shirt off, he came out in shorts and flip-flops, yelling at the girl that Stanton had just spoken to.

"I told you no fucking disturbances, you dumb whore."

"Sorry, Randy. He said he was—"

"I don't give a shit who he said he was. I said no disturbance. Maybe you have too much fucking cum in your ears?"

He smacked her lightly on the back of the head.

Stanton felt anger swell inside him. He looked to the girl as she sheepishly turned away and disappeared into the back. If he had called the police, he had a feeling her version of events would be different than his.

For the first time that he could remember, Stanton actually

wished Gunn was here with him.

"What the fuck do you want?" Randy said.

"My name is Jon Stanton," he said, rising, "I'm investigating the death of Jill Bonnie. I was told you were dating."

"Yeah? And who the fuck told you that?"

"Is it true?"

He waved his hand dismissively in Stanton's face. "You interrupt my shoot to talk about that cunt? I'm done talkin'. Go find my lawyer." He turned to leave.

"Mr. Jackson, the person that killed her is targeting porn stars. I believe you are a porn star. He's already taken someone close to you."

"The news said he only kills women."

"We don't release everything to the news." Stanton took a step closer. "You're right, though. He probably wouldn't kill you. With you, he'd be driven by jealousy. He would probably just castrate you and take your genitals as a souvenir."

Randy turned back around. "You're bullshitting me."

"It's what I would do if I were him."

Randy paused. "Hurry the fuck up and ask what you're gonna ask."

"Where were you on February eighth, the day she disappeared?"

"On vacation in Mexico. You can check with Southwest."

Stanton had already confirmed the trip. Though most of the public was unaware, a police database commonly referred to as PALS—Police Automated Locations Search—contained information regarding the location of every United States citizen. It was developed as a counterterrorism tool under the Bush Administration and had been slowly leaked to law enforcement agencies.

Childs had run a PALS search on Randy G. Jackson and the trip to Cabo San Lucas had been confirmed on the date Jill Bonnie had gone missing.

"Was she dating anyone else that you know of?"

"She was a whore, man. All these girls are. They think 'cause they do it on camera it ain't whoring but it is. They trade sex for money. She was fucking at least ten different guys. Coulda been any of 'em."

"How did she start in this business?"

"Her dad, man."

"What d'you mean?"

"Her dad's an asshole. He's some evangelical Jesus freak. She was never allowed to do nothing so when she turned eighteen she bailed to become an actress."

Stanton noticed bruising on the two knuckles of his right hand. "What happened to your hand?"

"Nothin'. Got pissed and hit a wall. We done? I gotta get back to fucking this bitch."

"Yeah, we're done."

Stanton walked out of the building and made a few notes on his phone. He would have to verify with the hotel in Cabo whether Randy was actually there. He clearly had a violent temper and a disdain for women. Since he worked within the porn industry, it would make sense for his co-stars to be the first victims. But his pathology indicated a rage killing. That would fit the ferocity of Nina Blum's murder, but not those of the other victims, who actually worked in the porn industry. Their deaths were meticulous and bloodless. Stanton couldn't picture someone like Randy having the patience to complete something like that.

It was evening by the time Stanton arrived at the restaurant. It was a favorite of his, a large shack set on the beach. The seafood was fresh, and fixed in between San Diego and Los Angeles off the freeway, it was never as packed as it should've been.

He walked in and saw Emma sitting in a booth by the windows overlooking the ocean. He sat down across from her and smiled as she took a sip of her drink.

"I've driven past here hundreds of times and never stopped," she said.

"Not many people know about it."

"That table over there, do you see it, with the four people?"

"Yeah."

"See that guy on the right? That's Louis CK. That comedian."

"Celebrities like this place. There're never that many people here, so they can actually feel normal for a while. I saw Tom Cruise here once."

"Mm, I had the biggest crush on him in high school. It was right after Top Gun came out. Who'd you have a crush on?"

"No one."

"No one? Not even Farrah Fawcett or Madonna or anyone like that?"

"No, I wasn't really interested in girls until much later in my life."

The waiter came and they ordered clams for appetizers and several smaller dishes to share. Stanton stared out at the ocean a long while before speaking.

"We have a unique bond with the ocean. I feel sorry for people that can't at least see it every day."

"I've always been scared of it. The unknown I guess. You never know what's lurking beneath you."

"It's the same in life." He looked at her. "Emma, I wanted to tell you something. I don't know if it explains anything or if it's an excuse or what—but I thought you should know."

She put her elbows on the table. "What is it?"

"I told you I'm an only child but that's not technically true. I had a sister. Liz. She was older than me by three years. When I was twelve, she was kidnapped from a movie theater." Stanton had to pause a moment. "They never found her."

"Holy shit. Jon, why didn't you ever tell me?"

"I've only told two other people and that's my ex-wife and my therapist. My kids don't even know."

"How...did it happen?"

"He just grabbed her. Liz was standing with a group of friends and they said some guy pulled up and asked them for directions. He was speaking really softly and Liz leaned in too close. He grabbed her and pulled her through the driver-side window and sped away."

"Did they ever find him?"

"No. I just…it's something that's always there for me. When I looked at Kyle Bonnie, I saw my father's face. He was a psychiatrist. After Liz, I was thrown into a deep depression. I was close to her. She was the one that taught me how to surf when we were on vacation in Maui once. I couldn't snap out of it. I wouldn't get out of bed. I couldn't go to school or even watch television. My father was completely helpless. I'd hear my mom crying at night because they thought they had lost me too."

"How'd you get out of it?"

"We moved. We moved down here to San Diego. My father thought the ocean and the sunshine would pull me out of it and it did. I also became a convert to the Mormon Church and relying on God and the sense of community helped me too. But I don't know how much of a recovery it was. I still think about Liz every single day of my life. Three or four or five times a day. I picture her on that surfboard in Maui showing me what to do. I see her reading me stories at night in my dreams. I can hear her voice sometimes at night and I get up and look around my apartment, but no one's ever there."

Emma sat quietly, her hand covering his. Her eyes had teared up, and as she was about to say something, the waiter came with the appetizers and set them on the table. She wiped her tears with the back of her napkin, careful not to smear her make-up.

"I don't even know what to say. I had no idea. I'm sorry I ever made you choose between me and your work."

He shook his head. "It's not my work anymore. I know I can never be a policeman again. But this was a case we started. One that Eli took away from me. What if there're more girls out there? Ones that would be with their families right now instead of buried in some canyon or floating in some river if Eli hadn't been the detective assigned? Or if I had seen him for what he was before that? I feel responsible for these girls."

"Jon, you are not—"

"Intellectually I know. I know it's not my fault and that Eli had everyone fooled. But emotionally I *feel* responsible. I can't make that feeling go away. I can only compensate for it. I can try to make peace with it."

"Do you really think meeting Philip Oster is going to bring you peace?"

"No, but maybe it will for Kyle Bonnie."

She nodded. "I understand. You do what you have to do."

Stanton hesitated. "Will you…"

"I'm not going anywhere. I missed you too much anyway. But promise me one thing: after the interview, you're done."

"I promise. Just the interview."

Stanton smiled as he held her hand. He looked out over the ocean. The moon was coming up as the sun set and darkness began to fall.

CHAPTER 16

Detective Stephen Gunn sped down Highway 15 in his new Corvette at over a hundred miles an hour. At one in the morning, traffic was almost nonexistent. He blared Alice in Chains and took sips out of a bottle of Amaretto. The alcohol was making his head feel warm and light and he caught himself with a dopey grin on his face.

He'd been to Encinitas several times but the beauty of the coastal town was never lost on him. He swooped through residential streets until coming to a modern house with white exterior walls and a red Spanish-tile roof. A gate surrounded the home and he pressed the call button.

"Yes?" a female voice responded.

"Stephen Gunn."

"Oh, yes. Come right in, Officer Gunn."

"Detective."

"Excuse me?"

"It's Detective Gunn. I haven't been an officer for six years."

"Okay, Detective. I'm sorry. I'll open the gates."

The gates slowly opened and he pulled through. In the small parking lot off to the side of the house, he parked between a BMW and a truck before finishing off the bottle of Amaretto and getting out.

A young blond in a negligée answered the door. She led him back to the living room where pornography was playing on a large flatscreen. Another man was sitting on the couch and Gunn lowered himself into the leather chair. The blond brought out his favorite drink, Coke and Jack, and he sipped it as he watched two lesbians on the screen.

"You come here that often? It's my first time," the other man said.

"Mind your own fuckin' business."

The man cleared his throat and turned away without responding. Gunn finished his drink and guessed he was too drunk to get an erection. He would have to rely on other things to arouse him tonight.

A brunette in fishnet stockings came out. "Stephen, it's good to see you again."

Gunn rose and followed the girl up a set of winding stairs to the top floor. Every room in the house except for the living room and kitchen had been converted into a bedroom and they walked into the farthest one on the right and shut the door.

The lights were dim and a bed with a black canopy took up most of the space. A sex swing, meant for a woman to sit on in a spread-eagle position, hung in the corner. Various sex toys lined the counters and shelves. Gunn took off his jacket and boots.

"I'm too drunk for fucking," he said.

"Oh. So what would you like to do?"

"You know what I want, Chelsea. Don't bullshit me."

The girl sat down on the edge of the bed. "I don't know. Last time I had to go to the emergency room."

Gunn reached into his pocket and pulled out a wad of hundred dollar bills. He began throwing them one at a time at her until a grin came over her face, right around two thousand. He threw her another thousand and then took off his pants, revealing silk boxers. Reaching down, he grabbed her by the back of the neck and pulled her near him before sticking his tongue into her mouth.

Suddenly, he pulled away and slapped her hard enough that she flew to her side. She yelped, but didn't complain. He then, gently, began kissing her on the cheek he had slapped.

As he raised his hand to do it again, he heard groaning coming from the bedroom next door and stopped.

"I told you not to have those bedrooms occupied when I'm

here," he said.

"I know. But he's a big client and demanded to see China Doll. I'm sorry."

Gunn sat up, about to scold her, when he noticed something about the voice in the other room. "Who is that?"

"We're not allowed to say."

"That sounds like J.J. Is that a man named J.J.? Black with a shaved head?"

The girl didn't respond.

Gunn ran out and neared the room next door. He slowly turned the knob and peeked inside. An Asian woman sat on top of a man on the bed, riding him and moaning. Gunn let his eyes adjust but he still couldn't make out the man. Except for a tattoo on his leg: an eagle holding a rifle. Gunn smiled.

"J.J.!" he said, opening the door.

The woman gasped and yelled for him to get out. Gunn walked over and leaned against a dresser. "Don't get all worked up, China Doll. Me and J.J., we go way back. Don't we?"

"Hey, Stephen, man, how you doin'?" he said nervously. "I been tryin' to get in touch with you, man."

"Really? That's funny 'cause I been here. Haven't moved or changed cell numbers as far as I know." He looked to the woman. "See, J.J. and I have this business relationship. I let him sell his poison on the corners in this neighborhood, and he gives me a cut. That is our relationship, isn't it, J.J.?"

J.J. didn't say anything.

"See 'cause that's the relationship I have with people all over this fuckin' city. But funny thing is, J.J. ain't been paying me. You believe that, China Doll? What if a client didn't pay you after sex? What would you do?"

"Call Tony," she whispered.

"What's that? I couldn't hear you."

"I would call Tony."

"That's right," Gunn said, "you would call Tony. And Tony's a big Samoan with a .45 tucked into his pants, isn't he?"

"Yeah."

"And he'd bust that client up if they didn't pay."

"Yeah."

"You see that, J.J.? China Doll, a two-dollar whore past her prime, would have you busted up if you didn't pay. Now what do you think a homicide detective you didn't pay should do?"

"Hey, man, it ain't like that. Times is rough like leather, yo. People not be payin' me and I just ain't got the green to be kickin' up to nobody. I ain't even got enough for my own chronic, ya know?"

"Really? China Doll, how much did you charge J.J.?"

"I can't say," she whispered.

"We're all friends here, don't worry. Now how much?"

She swallowed. "Seven hundred."

"Seven hundred dollars. Now J.J., you owe me two Gs. That seven hundred could've been a nice little payment to keep me happy."

J.J. sat up. He stood next to the bed and reached for his pants. China Doll stood next to him. "Yo, I got a little bit right here, lemmie get it."

Gunn stepped over to make sure he wasn't reaching for a piece. As he did so, J.J. grabbed China Doll by the shoulders and threw her into him, her head cracking into his nose. J.J. leapt for the open window. He dove headfirst outside, sliding down the shingles and twisting around, falling onto his feet.

Gunn threw the woman out of the way and sprinted for the stairs. He jumped them several at a time until he got outside. He saw J.J. making a sprint for the BMW. Gunn pulled out his firearm and slipped on the silencer. He fired twice, shattering the windshield with one of the shots. J.J. instinctively ducked and then ran around the house. Gunn followed.

He turned the corner and J.J.'s fist slammed into his chin, sending him onto his back. J.J. kicked him in the head several times before taking off running again. Gunn sat up, roaring in anger as he aimed his weapon and fired for the man's legs. He missed.

Gunn jumped into his car and peeled out, speeding down the

street. He could see J.J.'s outline as the man sprinted through bushes and gardens and lawns. He turned up a driveway and hopped a fence into the backyard. Gunn slammed on the brakes and spun the car around. He shot up a street heading north as J.J. jumped another fence onto the sidewalk. Gunn ran the car over the curb right behind him, slamming into his backside, and sending him up onto the hood and over the car.

He stepped out and went to the trunk to retrieve a baseball bat he kept there. Tapping the wooden bat against the concrete, he walked over to where J.J. was lying on his back, staring up to the sky and groaning in pain.

"A couple grand," Gunn said, standing over him. "You went through all this for just a couple grand? Why didn't you just pay me?"

"'Cause you's a muthafucka. That's why."

Gunn squatted down. "Am I not threatenin' enough? Did you think you'd get away with it? What?"

J.J. was silent a while before he said, "You ain't never happy, man."

"What d'you mean?"

"No matter how much green you get, you ain't never full. Your belly's always hungry. I pay you a G and you want two. I'll give you two and you want three. Ain't no end in it, man."

Gunn nodded and stood up. "Interesting. That's pretty profound insight for a drug dealing piece a shit like you."

He scoffed. "You got the biggest take and the badge. Who's the piece a shit?"

Gunn grinned, and raised the bat over his head.

CHAPTER 17

The District Attorney's Office was nearly empty by 8:00 p.m. as Stanton came through the doors. The security guard at the front desk checked him in and asked for his sidearm.

"I don't have one," Stanton said.

"What kinda cop doesn't carry a gun?"

"A retired one," Stanton said, walking to the elevator.

As he stepped off the elevator and headed for the Special Prosecutions section, he saw Stephen Gunn sitting on a leather sofa, reading an issue of *Sports Illustrated.* He didn't notice Stanton so Stanton got to observe him.

Gunn appeared much older than he did even a year ago. His hair had more gray and the small wrinkles by his eyes were more pronounced. He'd always been good looking, but in the way that many people considered Sylvester Stallone good looking: he had a kind of boxer's handsomeness.

Gunn finally felt his presence and lowered the magazine. The two men looked at each other a moment before speaking.

"You look tan," Gunn said. "You look tanner every time I see you."

"I need to wear more sunscreen. Even the best brands lose their effectiveness after a couple hours. The salt in the ocean scrubs it off."

"I tried surfing a few times. Didn't really like it. Boogie boarding was more fun. You don't fall as much."

Stanton shrugged and sat down across from him in a chair. He put his feet on a footstool and leaned back to appear relaxed and at ease.

"How's your ex?" Gunn asked. "Melissa, right?"

"Yeah. She's fine. She married a football player. Someone from the Chargers but he got traded to another team."

"You miss her?"

"Yeah, I miss her a lot. Being a cop cost me my marriage. And all the time I've lost with my boys." He paused. "It really bothers me."

"Especially at night," Gunn said.

"Yeah."

"I've had two marriages both end in the worst ways possible, and you know what I learned, Johnny? I learned that people are basically alone. No matter how close you get to someone else, you're still alone. That don't bode well for marriage."

"I disagree. We're social animals set up to have mates. There's some debate about whether men are designed to practice monogamy or to have as many partners as possible, but there's no question that we need other people. Deprived of people, even for short periods, people begin to display symptoms of psychosis almost immediately."

"Guys," Kathleen said, turning the corner, "sorry to keep you waiting. Come on back."

Stanton followed Gunn as the two men walked down the hallway to Kathleen Ackerman's office. Stanton sat across from her as Gunn chose to go stand by the window.

"Well, boys, I wanted to meet with the two of you to go through tomorrow's interview." She pulled a file out of the stack on her desk. "This is Oster's biographical information. Some good stuff but nothing you wouldn't expect."

Gunn said, "It's not like we need to know that much about him."

"What do you mean?" Kathleen asked.

"He's a sick fuck. They're all sick fucks. You don't need to know much more than that."

"Some of them are, like you said, Steve, sick fucks, but most of them are just sick. You dig into their backgrounds and they've had monstrous upbringings. Doesn't excuse what they do at all, but it helps me understand it."

Gunn shook his head and stared out the window to the street below. "The liberal bullshit psychobabble's got to you too, huh, Kathy? There ain't no cause for what they do." Gunn leaned against the wall, folding his arms. He was still looking out the window. "One of the first cases I had, we busted this pimp. A girl of his, nice girl about fifteen-years-old, kept some of the money that was supposed to go to him so that she could buy her five-year-old son a birthday present. He smacked her around real good and she came to us.

"We followed her back to the pimp's house and made an arrest." Gunn smiled. "Dude was so drunk he took a swing at me and missed by about three feet. He fell and broke his nose on the cement of his porch.

"So we cuff him and go inside to secure the house. And this was some fucking house. Pool and hot tub in the back. Big screen, bearskin rugs, the works. We're goin' through this house from room to room and I hear crying. It's coming from the basement. I run down there. It's really dark and I'm searching for a light, running my hands along the walls, and this crying is louder. It's definitely coming from a room in the basement.

"I couldn't find a light so I take out my flashlight and start lookin' around. There's a buncha junk down there and the crying's coming from a little hallway. I run up there and break down the door and inside are four kids chained to a radiator. They're just dirty, man. Covered in shit and piss and just scared. The youngest one was five. Turns out our pimp was takin' his girls' kids and punishing 'em whenever the girls didn't earn enough. He'd starve 'em or beat 'em, whatever."

Gunn took a deep breath and exhaled slowly, as if calming himself.

"And there's this little guy of like seven and he ain't afraid. He stands up and asks who we are. I tell him the police and he says his name's Rick. I get my partner to come down with the kids and we call it in and I'm upstairs alone with the pimp. I've never wanted to put a cap into somebody's head as much as I did his. Not before or since. But I didn't. I testified in court against him and he went away for twenty. But I followed Rick. This was like nine years ago so I got to see him become a teenager. He would send me birthday cards and we'd even talk on the phone sometimes. I took him out to Disneyland a couple a times 'cause I knew his mom couldn't afford it."

Gunn turned and looked at them. "When Rick was twelve-years-old, he locked one of his classmates, a little girl, in the janitor's closet at school and raped her. When he was done, he tried to suffocate her by putting a bag over her head but he didn't hold it long enough and she just passed out. That's humanity. That's what I got when I was kind and caring. People are animals. If you treat 'em like they're not, they'll bite you for it."

Stanton and Kathleen stared in silence as Gunn walked over and lay down on the couch. Though he and Gunn had grown close when they were partners, Stanton had never heard that story before. Stanton had a similar experience with children locked in a basement and he would've liked sharing that with Gunn back then. Not now. Now, Gunn was a jaded mass of anger and frustration.

"Do you know anything about the apostle Paul?" Stanton asked.

"Holy shit, you're really gonna give a sermon right now? Save that shit for church."

"Paul's not just interesting for religious reasons. He's one of the most interesting men in history, even in a secular sense. He grew up a Pharisee and when Christianity was blooming he was one of the persecutors. Modern Christians don't talk about how evil he really was in his persecutions. He would routinely torture and execute Christians. One of his favorite things to do was torture them to the point that they'd almost pass out and then tell them to renounce Christ. But he was also highly intelligent. He understood that most Christians would rather become martyrs than do that. So he would stop torturing them and bring in their wives and make the husbands watch as he tortured them. He knew most men couldn't tolerate that.

"But a single experience on a road changed him. For the rest of his life, he gave up all his possessions and just travelled from town to town, preaching love and peace until his death. He was hated and beaten and tortured himself because of his past, but he endured it all because he knew change was possible. People might have horrible inclinations, but they can change."

Gunn shook his head. "I ain't seen it."

Kathleen shifted in her chair. "This is fascinating, it really is, but I'd like to get home soon if that's okay with you guys."

"Of course," Stanton said. "Sorry."

Gunn said, "No war stories, Kathy? You usually love bull-shitting with the badges."

"I've got a few myself. But I'm exhausted. I've been in trial almost two weeks now."

"I saw that," Stanton said. "On the news. The actor, right? He allegedly shot his wife to death outside a restaurant."

"There's no allegedly about it. He did it, but juries have been less and less inclined to convict celebrities over the years. Any-way, Jon, I really do appreciate this. I'm not bullshitting. I mean that." She handed him the file. "It's Oster's background."

Stanton opened the file and began reading.

CHAPTER 18

Philip Reginald Oster was born in Connecticut on December 7, 1963. His mother, from what they could tell, was unemployed and his father was out of the picture. Oster had had a few stints with the foster-care system, and reading the Department of Child Services notes, Stanton gathered that it was due to his mother's drug addiction and frequent prostitution charges. Physical abuse was noted, including broken ribs when he was nine and several broken fingers and toes.

When he was thirteen, his mother died under unusual circumstances in a home accident. Oster was the only one home with her at the time. He was briefly interviewed as a suspect and stated that his mother had fallen off a ladder while trying to change a lightbulb and hit her head on the kitchen counter. The police were unable to contradict this story and so charges were never brought against him. Forensics in the seventies was not what it is now. Stanton had no doubt that if they had even a mediocre crime scene unit back then, they would have found Oster responsible.

After his mother's death, Oster was placed permanently into foster care. He bounced from one house to the next. Though there were no notes about his behavior, the frequency of his moves told Stanton that he couldn't last long with any family. Only one other note followed: a brief description of Oster's frequent night urinations and his inability to stop.

The Child Services report ended and various police reports and criminal histories began, a thick stack of paper filling the middle of the file, each sheet stamped CONFIDENTIAL IN-

FORMATION. DISSEMINATION TO ANYONE OTHER THAN RE-QUESTER WILL RESULT IN PROSECUTION. It was Oster's juvenile criminal history.

The charges began small, when he was eleven: petty theft and underage drinking. But they escalated quickly. By thirteen he had his first assault charge, one of fourteen assault charges he would gather before even being old enough to drive. By sixteen, he had a rap sheet filled with crimes ranging from burglary and car theft to assault with a deadly weapon, animal cruelty, and arson. The cruelty charges stuck out to Stanton. Most psychopaths began with animals, particularly dogs and cats as they can respond to pain in an almost human-like fashion. That, coupled with setting fires and frequent night urination, was a trait nearly every serial murderer had in common in childhood.

By the time Oster reached adulthood, he had already spent half his life in juvenile detention centers, which were not much different from adult jails.

He dropped out of high school at the age of fifteen and worked at a mechanic shop until he was old enough to apply to the police academy. Stanton saw six applications, all denied. He failed both the physical and written exams each time.

"What do you think?" Kathleen finally said. She glanced over to Gunn who was soundly asleep on her couch. "Don't think your partner's going to be much help."

"He certainly has the early childhood indicators. They call it the triumvirate: night urination, setting fires, and the torture of animals. But I would guess he has an extremely low IQ. That doesn't seem to fit the pattern for how he handled the victims except Nina Blum."

"Why her?"

"There was a lot of evidence left behind. Semen, saliva, shoeprints…none of that was left with the other victims that we have bodies for. Nina Blum was also a housewife, not a porn star. They were committed by two different people."

"Why would he be taking responsibility for all of them?"

"He could be covering for a partner. In cases like this, with two or more sadists committing crimes together, there's always a dominant and submissive personality. If he's the submissive, he might cover for his dominant partner, but he's more likely to give him up out of a sense of inferiority. If he's the dominant, there's no way he would take responsibility for another's crimes. He would degrade them instead, trying to make everyone think it was sloppy work and far inferior to his."

Kathleen picked up a pencil and tapped it a few times against the desktop before turning it over and over in her hand. "So you think he's definitely telling the truth and someone else out there helped him commit at least some of these?"

"There is one other possibility: multiple personality disorder."

"Oh come on, you've got to be kidding me. Don't even mess around with that. You're going to give his attorney a field day."

"It's a possibility we can't rule out. I've had several cases where the defendants suffered from MPD and didn't even realize they were committing crimes. They would wake up in their houses, covered in blood, and have no idea where it came from. It's a complete fragmentation of the mind. One portion has no idea what the other portion is doing. It would be perfectly consistent with Oster's diagnosis for him to have committed all the murders and for Nina Blum to simply have been another personality. The one problem is, he wouldn't have remembered any of the details."

She shook her head. "Too far fetched. I met Oster when we tried to convince him to confess without you. He didn't seem crazy to me."

"You wouldn't be able to tell. Even he wouldn't know what he was doing."

"I don't buy it. I think he's got a partner or a copycat and for some reason he wants to confess. Maybe his partner's in custody and about to give him up so he wants to beat him to the punch?"

"Maybe."

She exhaled. "I was thinking I would gather all the information. I've basically got a direct examination written and I was going to take him through the murders one by one. I'd like to do it chronologically but unless you can give me a clue on the order without bodies, there's no way."

Stanton shook his head. "Whoever was first is going to get you the most important information from him."

"Why?"

"The first in a series is usually someone they see frequently that they already know or have at least introduced themselves to. Someone from work or church or living in the same apartment complex or something. If there is a partner, he likely would've participated in the first one. Sometimes the victim is killed during a consensual sexual encounter and they get a taste for it after that. Once people see that lightning doesn't come down and strike them after they kill, they don't have the same moral dilemmas anymore."

"Well, I'll make sure to hit on that a lot. Is there anything else you want me to ask him?"

He shook his head. "I don't think he's going to be very cooperative. He's angry at the police, and jealous. He's not going to want to cooperate with us either. Chances are he only wants me there so he can gloat that I never managed to catch him."

"I don't think so."

Stanton could see she was holding back. "You seem pretty confident."

"I am."

He paused. "There's something you're not telling me."

"It's not your concern, Jon."

"I'm here as a favor. I think I should know everything that's going on."

She twirled the pencil a few times and then placed it down on the desk. "We struck a plea deal with Oster."

"What deal?"

"He confesses, we take the death penalty off the table. We got it in writing. His attorney—Henry Grimes—signed off on it." She was silent a moment. "Are you upset?"

"No."

"Really? Usually when I do something like this with a scumbag like Oster the detectives stop returning my calls."

"I don't believe in the death penalty."

"That's an odd stance for a homicide detective."

"Is it? I don't think it's odd at all. We're showing them that society isn't the cold-hearted monster these people think it is."

"Hm. Is that what Stephen is going to say too?"

"I don't know what he's thinking," Stanton said, looking over to Gunn. "He's always been a mystery to me."

She nodded and stood up, stretching her back and neck. "Unless you have questions for him you want to go over, that's pretty much all I need. I'm just doing the examination and coming back the next day if we don't get to everything."

Stanton rose. "I don't think he'll respond well to a woman. Especially an attractive one." Stanton saw her blush and wasn't sure why until he realized what he'd said. "I mean, he's patterning the selected victims after someone in his life. Probably his mother but easily a wife or girlfriend that triggered this episode. I don't think he'll be receptive to women."

She waved her hand dismissively. "I've dealt with plenty of psychos. He'll crack a few tit jokes and then we'll get past it. I'll be fine."

CHAPTER 19

Stanton woke early and went for a jog on the beach. The sun was coming up and the sky burned a light pink. He took his shoes off and did wind sprints in the wet sand where the surf was just starting to come in.

Exhausted, he walked back toward his car and viewed the full sunrise, watching its rays break on the surface of the ocean. A few surfers were out but the waves were mediocre and they soon lost interest and went back to their cars to get loaded.

Stanton looked around for Ione, but didn't see her. He drove back to his apartment. Even though he'd been living alone in apartments for several years, it still felt odd not to come to a home and have anyone greet him at the door. He'd thought about buying a dog for the past few months but had never gotten around to it.

After showering and shaving, he changed and left. He took out his cell phone on the drive to the prison to call Emma but decided he didn't want to talk to her right now. He didn't want her fresh on his mind as he went where he was about to go.

The George Bailey Maximum Security Correctional Complex looked like any other prison: concrete and steel. The environment was sterile, meant to portray orderliness. But just inside, past the brick walls, was little more than a jungle.

A jail housed inmates that had less than a year sentence or were awaiting court dates and couldn't afford bail. The turnover was so high and frequent that relationships weren't established. As a consequence, violence was relatively low and sexual assaults extremely uncommon.

But prisons housed the worst offenders. The ones who were unaffected by frequent jail stays and continued to commit crimes. Or first offenders that had committed crimes so grievous the state didn't feel anywhere else was appropriate.

Prison had a hierarchy and the inmates had to live by an established set of laws. If these laws were broken, punishment was given by those inmates that ran the facility.

Stanton had once done research on a grant from the Bureau of Prisons on the corruption of the prison guards and what he'd found was staggering. In some states, corruption was nearly non-existent. But others, like Louisiana and New Jersey, had a high number of prison guards that went into the profession solely for the opportunity to skim the inmates' profits.

Drugs were in high demand in prison, and that need had to be met. The guards would help the inmates get the drugs inside and then get paid a share of the profit. Female prostitution was also common in the conjugal visits trailers, but much more difficult to pull off. So inmates frequently engaged in homosexual assault. Stanton had found that 40% of inmates admitted to being the victims of at least one sexual assault. He guessed that number was closer to double that but that many of the participants in his study lied to protect their image of masculinity.

Stanton went into the main lobby of chrome surfaces and concrete walls. He checked in and sat down on a bench. The guards would glance at him every once in a while and murmur to each other, but for the most part they treated him with the respect they would give a detective.

After ten minutes of reading Facebook posts on his iPhone, Stanton saw Gunn and Kathleen coming through the door. He wondered if they had driven together or just happened to arrive at the same time.

"You ready?" Kathleen said to him as he rose and began to follow her through the metal doors that lead to the visitation rooms.

"Sure."

Stanton was silent as they walked down the long corridor

with no windows. Gunn wasn't wearing a suit though wearing one was customary for interviews. It helped establish dominance. Instead he wore tattered designer jeans and a leather jacket with the collar flipped up. Stanton had not worn a suit either in an attempt to seem more relatable.

The visitation room was cleared except for a table. Only one of the rooms had a window, from what Stanton remembered, and they'd been given that one. Stanton had suggested it might relax Oster. Outside was a single tree, beyond that a fifteen-foot, double-twined, electrified chain-link fence topped with razor wire.

Sitting down in a semi-circle with an empty chair across the table, the three of them remained quiet. Stanton leaned his elbows on the table and looked out to the tree. Gunn flipped through his Android and sighed. Kathleen was tapping her ring finger against the table.

"You fidget when you're nervous," Stanton said to Kathleen.

She looked down to the ring and stopped.

"This is a big case," Gunn said. "She fucks it up, it's her ass."

"My bosses support me a hundred percent," she said, somewhat offended.

"Until those convictions slip. Those convictions start slipping and we'll see how much they support you then."

An automatic door opened nearby followed by a metal door on the other side of the room. Two deputies walked in with the prisoner between them.

Philip Oster was in a white jumpsuit with blue laceless shoes. He wore glasses and his graying hair was long enough to touch the tips of his shoulders. The chains on his ankles were tight and he shuffled in rather than walked. On both forearms were tattoos of big-bosomed women.

Oster was sat at the table and one of the deputies said, "If you get up without me telling you to, you gonna get Tased in the back."

"Understood," Oster said. His voice was high, almost feminine. He grinned and said, "Detective Jon Stanton. I've heard a lot about you."

Stanton didn't respond at first. He waited for Kathleen to show she was running this interview by interjecting, but she didn't.

"I understand you wanted to meet me," Stanton said. "You should know, I'm not a detective anymore."

"Oh, I know."

"I have no power to influence any plea bargains," Stanton said.

"I don't care. My attorney's taken care of that. By the way, where is that fat piece a shit?"

"He should be here shortly," Kathleen said. "I don't want to begin until he's here."

"Suit yourself," Oster said. "I'd really rather talk to Jon here. Ain't that right, Jon? You and me, we got a lot in common."

"Such as?"

"No, not right now. Not with these two here. But you know what I mean. You know everything."

"Mr. Oster, I think my being here is—"

The door opened and another deputy presented Henry Grimes. He was sweating, wearing a button-down shirt with pit stains. He held his sports-coat in his arm and pulled out a handkerchief to pat his brow. Though he appeared disheveled and wore old clothing, Stanton knew Grimes' watch cost more than Stanton's car. It was the one frivolity Grimes allowed himself.

He sat down next to Oster and didn't say anything. He pulled out a digital recorder as Kathleen did the same and they both hit the record button nearly simultaneously.

"This is a Harold B. Grimes, bar number 54428. I'm here with Philip Oster at the George Bailey prison, negotiating a plea bargain in Mr. Oster's case."

"This is Kathleen Ackerman from the San Diego County District Attorney's Office, bar number 111722. I'm here solely in a supervisory role. With me are Detective Stephen Gunn and Jonathan Stanton, who's here at Mr. Oster's request and solely at Mr. Oster's request. The date is—"

"I'm gettin' bored," Oster interrupted. "Johnny, are you gettin' bored?" Stanton didn't reply. "I think I would like this much better without the suits and the asshole in the leather jacket. Yeah, I would definitely like this better without them."

"Phil," Grimes said, "we talked about this. This is the best thing."

"You know, I ain't never really liked none a the lawyers I had. Necessary evil, though, so people like this cunt here don't steamroll me. Ain't that right, cunt?"

"Phil!" Grimes yelped. "What the hell do you think you're doing?"

"It's all right," Kathleen said calmly. "Mr. Oster, I'm tolerating this as best I can. It took some doing to bring Mr. Stanton in on this. If you don't wish to cooperate, I'd be happy to withdraw our plea deal and seek the death penalty."

"Death penalty with what, darlin'? Your tits? You ain't got shit. If I don't talk you gotta go back to your boss and explain to him why a serial killer got away. I don't expect he'd be none too thrilled."

"Excuse us a moment," she said. She rose and walked to the other end of the room. Gunn and Stanton followed. "Well, it's up to you, Jon. I won't ask you to be alone with this freak. If you don't wanna do it, just tell me. He's in here for at least twenty before a parole hearing so a lot can happen in that time. I'm not too worried about him. But the victims' families would want us to follow up on this."

Gunn said, "Fuck him. Let's walk."

"No," Stanton said, "it's fine. Leave your recorder on. I don't think Henry expected this either. This wasn't premeditated. It could be what we need to get him to relax and speak openly."

She looked to Oster who made an obscene gesture with his tongue. "Fine. But we'll be right outside the door. One of the guards will be in the room too."

"I don't think he wants to hurt me. Not in here anyway."

She nodded. "Be careful."

The two of them walked out as Grimes stood up and said

loudly, "I just want it noted for the record that this is a bad idea and I object to it but am following through at the request of my client."

"Don't worry, counselor," Oster said, "I ain't filin' no bar complaints from in here."

The three of them exited, leaving Stanton to stare at the man seated at the table. He walked over and sat down, putting his hands in his pockets with the thumbs out. Keeping the thumbs out portrayed a sense of confidence as opposed to when one hid the whole hand. Stanton did this purposely to hide the uneasiness he felt bubbling in his gut.

"Never liked lawyers," Oster said. "Have you?"

"There're some good ones. Our Founding Fathers were lawyers."

He nodded. "Yeah, guess so. But ain't seem to ever find the good ones. That tubby bastard is chargin' me thirty grand just to set up a deal. You believe that? You know any other profession that can charge that much for something so simple?"

"Bankers and doctors," Stanton said.

"Guess you're right. Can't be too pissed at him anyway. He got you here."

"I came here because I want to hear your story."

"Why?"

"I'm curious about you. You have an interesting take on life. I think it'd be shameful if we didn't get that down on record."

"Hm. You're as good as everybody was sayin'. Even had me buyin' the horseshit. Flattery's hard to overcome, ain't it?"

Stanton suddenly got the impression that his initial analysis of Oster had been wrong: there was intelligence there. Covered by a thick layer of uncontrollable aggression.

"So," Stanton said, "it's your dime. What would you like to talk about?"

CHAPTER 20

"I'd like to talk about Nehor Stark," Oster said.

Stanton inadvertently held his breath. That was a name he had tried for over a year to forget and it had come up twice in one week. "What would you like to say about him?"

"I'm curious if you've visited him at the hospital? I heard he's doin' really well in his therapy."

"I haven't."

"Don't it piss you off that a sick fucker like him might get out again one day? What kinda system we got when he can be out again among decent folk?"

"I don't think they'll ever let him out. The victims' families have all filed suits against the state over his release. I think he'll die in there."

Oster shrugged. "You never know. Ten years down the line everyone's forgotten…new people in places a power…"

"I'd like to talk about something else, Mr. Oster."

"I'm all ears."

"I'd like to speak about Jill Bonnie."

"Oh, yeah. She was a hot little number. You seen photos?"

"I have."

"She hot, ain't she?"

"Very attractive, yes. How did you meet her?"

"I get around. Yeah, you shoulda seen her at the last, boy. When she was beggin' me not to kill her. She woulda done anythin' to anybody to avoid that. I had her do some things too. Some things that shouldn't be mentioned in proper company such as yourself." He laughed. "Then I killed her anyway. You shoulda seen the surprise on her face. What'd she think I was gonna do? Keep my word? I'm a fuckin' criminal."

Stanton had to grip the table leg and squeeze until his hand hurt. "She was quite beautiful. Women like her aren't found every day. I'm a bit surprised you killed her and didn't keep her for a while."

"Oh I thought about it," Oster said, his leg beginning to manically bounce up and down. "But the bitch got brave. She started tryin' to run off. Eventually she woulda done it. See I kept her in a box under my bed. A perfect little toy to bring out whenever I wanted. She figured out how to get outta that box and I found her tryin' to get outta the house one day."

Stanton made a mental note that he said house and not condo or apartment. "But she was found in her bedroom."

"I took her back after it was all said and done. I ain't a monster. She needed to be at home."

"Why heroin?"

"That's what all them movie stars like. I thought it'd be a good way for them to go. Nice and sleepy. I told you, I ain't a monster."

"Why'd you select her?"

"You saw what she looked like."

"There're plenty of beautiful women in Southern California. That can't be the only reason."

"No, I guess it can't. Hell, I don't know. I just saw her and thought I had to have her."

"Did you see her in one of her films?"

He smiled. "I think I'd like to ask you a question now."

"Sure."

"You're Mormon, ain't you?"

"Yes," Stanton said.

"So you believe in God and Jesus and that horseshit, right?"

"Yes."

"People like me, do you believe we have a choice in what we do? Or is it just the devil?"

"I think you have a choice. But there're undeniably dark

forces in the world and they influence us."

He nodded. "So do you think I'm evil or sick?"

Stanton hesitated. "Evil."

"Why Jon Stanton, I can't remember a time a cop was honest with me about *everything*. You are as strange an asshole as I was told you are."

"After you killed Bonnie, how long did you wait for your second girl?"

"Few months. After that, you start gettin' the urge again, which I didn't expect, and it gets so that's all you can think about."

Stanton suppressed a grin. Jill Bonnie was the first victim.

"I'd like to take you through the other girls, Phil."

"No, no I just wanted to meet you today. Nothin' much else. Besides, you gonna be meetin' my partner again real soon."

"What do you mean?"

"I mean, he went on without me the selfish sonumbitch. You still got yourself work to do." He turned and looked to the guard. "I'm ready to go now."

"I'd like to spend more time with you."

"No, I think we're done."

"Phil, I find you very interesting and would really like it if you talked to me a little more. I don't get to meet such interesting people so often."

"Not right now. Maybe come back and see me, though."

Stanton stood up, his mind racing as to what to say as the guard helped Oster to his feet. He wasn't sure if he could ever get Oster to open up like this again.

"Goodbye, Detective. I'll see you soon."

It was one in the afternoon by the time Stanton got to the Mexican grill and joined Kathleen and Gunn on the patio. Two empty beer bottles were on the table along with chips and salsa and Stanton took a chip and dipped it in the thick, red liquid before taking a bite.

"That certainly didn't go as planned," Kathleen said.

"Finding out the first victim was the most important part. However he found her is how he found the other women."

"What did you guys make of his claiming he has a partner? Believable?"

Gunn shrugged. "Could be just messin' with us to make us spin our wheels."

"Is that your take, Jon?"

"I think he realizes I would find out pretty quickly if he has a partner. If I find out he's lying, I'm not going to trust him again and the game ends. That's what this is to him, a game. I think he enjoys the power he has over us right now."

Gunn said, "I still got connections in Vice. We can see if any porn stars have gone missing the past few months."

Kathleen looked to Stanton. "Are you going to follow through with this? I know you said you would just do the interview."

Stanton took another chip. "I promised someone that all I would do is the interview. I think I have to stop."

Stanton could barely get the words out. His guts were wound up so tight it was as if someone was clenching them in a fist. He wanted nothing more than to work this case. To go back to that prison and sit across from Oster and play this game. And that frightened him more than anything: that the game excited him just as much as it did Oster. It filled Stanton with a sense of shame and guilt. That was why he had initially said no, and why no one understood why he couldn't just do one interview or look at one file: the game would suck him in.

"Jon," Kathleen said, "this is your area. I'm not equipped to deal with people like this. I deal with juries and judges. I can't read this guy."

"Forget him," Gunn said, "I can do it without him."

Stanton took one more chip and then rose. "You'll have to. I'm sorry."

As he drove away, he looked into his rearview and saw Gunn place his hand over Kathleen's and lean in for a kiss. He had suspected they were sleeping together and wondered why they both hadn't tried to keep him working on this case.

CHAPTER 21

Stanton drove on the Santa Monica Freeway and watched the ocean in the distance as he climbed a small hill. The freeway was busy and several cars honked at him as he was driving just under the speed limit, but he didn't feel like going fast right now.

He passed a home to his right in a cul-de-sac that he had visited once as a detective. It was for a case in Special Victims that involved a homosexual rape at a bachelor party. Stanton had interviewed several people that attended the party but had never found a suspect. The victim had been drugged and couldn't give many details. Years later, Stanton had learned that the victim had killed himself.

He called Emma and told her what had happened at the interview.

"So what're you going to do?" she said.

"I'm going back to my practice tomorrow."

"And you're just going to forget about all this? Just like that?"

"What choice do I have? This is an investigation that could take months. I can't put my business on hold that long. Parents are relying on me to find their children."

"Isn't this kinda the same thing?"

"I thought you didn't want me working with the police anymore?"

"I don't, but I want it for the right reasons, Jon. I don't want you to always be thinking about this case and have it affect us."

"It won't."

"Well, if it does, just know I'm here for you either way."

"Thanks. I better go, this is my exit."

"Okay. Will I see you tonight?"

"Yeah, come over hungry. We're going to have a barbeque on the beach."

"I'm so excited. I've been looking forward to it all day."

"See you tonight."

"Bye."

The freeway thinned as Stanton got over to the right shoulder and took the exit leading to downtown. Twenty minutes later he was in front of a plush office building. He parked out front before walking inside. The receptionist was friendly and remembered his name. He signed in on a clipboard and then sat down as she said, "Dr. Palmer will be with you in a moment."

After ten minutes a thin blond woman in a suit stepped out of wooden double doors. A man preceded her. He looked anxious as he glanced at Stanton and then quickly away.

"Jon," the woman said, "glad you made it. Come in."

Two thick leather chairs took up the center of the room. Stanton followed her inside and sat down across from her. He didn't say anything as she made herself comfortable and smiled.

"So how's life?" she said.

"Good."

"Your work is going well?"

"It is. I've been a little sidetracked lately, but other than that, it's fine. I have more clients than I know what to do with. I've been having to refer them out."

"Sounds like you're where you want to be professionally."

"I never pictured myself as a private investigator, but yeah, things are going great professionally." Stanton glanced around the office and saw no photos, no identifying markers whatsoever. Only three degrees up on the wall and a medical license.

"And your personal life. I think we discussed in the last session that you're getting serious with a professor from UCLA."

"Yeah, Emma. She's fantastic. She's one of the smartest people I've ever known. A little awkward socially but in a very endearing way."

"Have you two been intimate yet?"

"Not in the way you're asking. I don't know if we ever discussed this, but I won't have sex outside of marriage. It's just something I don't believe in."

"We have discussed it, but you would be amazed how many men I have in that chair every week tell me their beliefs and then break them the next day. Sounds like your principles are very important to you."

"They are. Every man needs a code to live by and I have mine. If you don't have a code, you're just wandering aimlessly through life and you'll end up somewhere you don't want to be."

For some reason, Stanton thought of his father. His father had only science to live by, not a code that guided his actions. When Stanton was older, he noticed his father slip in and out of depression. Though he knew it was a genetic predisposition, lacking a guide to live by could have easily been a contributor.

"What does Emma think about your work?"

"She keeps hounding me to go back and be a professor. She thinks with my experience any university psychology department would snap me up."

"You are an expert in abnormal psychology if there ever was one. Do you think about going back into that field?"

"No. Not at all. Many professors escape from reality. They want to live in the little commune of universities and not have anything to do with real people or real work. I get to help people in a very direct way right now, a way that no professor ever could. The vast majority of my clients are parents who've had children kidnapped."

She nodded. "Do you think your sense of fulfillment in this area comes from what happened to your sister?"

"I don't know. I haven't consciously thought about it much."

"It's my understanding that very few children who go missing more than forty-eight hours are ever found. Is that true?"

"It is."

"So you say you're helping the parents, but what do you tell them when you can't find their children?"

"I explain up front how difficult it is and that the chances are slim. I'm never deceptive with them."

"What about with yourself?"

"What do you mean?"

"When you sign up a new case, do you tell yourself you're going to find this child?"

"In some sense, I do. I have to. If I thought every single child was a lost cause, I couldn't do it."

Palmer shifted in her chair. "Jon, we've never talked in depth about the disappearance of your sister. Would you feel comfortable speaking about that with me?"

"I guess."

"You told me you two were close."

"We were."

"When she disappeared, did your parents tell you right away what happened to her?"

"Yes. My father didn't believe in lying to children. When I was five, he sat us down and explained that Santa Claus and the Tooth Fairy and all the other things people celebrate on holidays are false. He believed in pure reason and didn't want us believing in any mythology or spirituality."

"How did that make you feel?"

"I think I would've been a happier child with it in my life. There's a lot of magic in childhood and to a large extent, he took that magic away. But he was doing what he thought was right for his children. I don't blame him for that."

"And how did he feel about you being a practicing Mormon?"

"He hated it. Not just 'cause it was Mormonism, he would've hated any religion I converted to. He thought religion was a crutch that weak people use to make them feel better about death."

"Did you believe that?"

"No. I saw what living a life of reason did to him. Reason's a tool, and a very good one, but we're creatures that are tuned to have myth and magic in our lives. Reason doesn't give meaning or purpose to anything. It's like the fangs on a snake or wings on a bird. They're meant for specific tasks and nothing else. I think if all religion were wiped out today, it would start up again in exactly the same way tomorrow. It's part of our psychology; we need it. Even people who think they don't need it and despise religion have religious tendencies toward things: like a love for the environment or animals. Those are all substitutes for religious thinking."

"You said you saw what a life of reason did to your father. What did it do to him?"

"He was distant from everything around him. He felt like the world was just made up of tools for man's use, and it's hard to find beauty or joy in tools. I never saw him laugh. Not once. I know he loved my mother, but I can't imagine that they had a happy marriage. He would've found absolute love irrational."

"How did he react after the disappearance of your sister?"

A memory Stanton had hidden deep in the recesses of his mind came flooding back. His father, a face of stone, simply accepting the disappearance of one of his children, and the single tear that he was unable to hold back. Rolling down his cheek and onto his chest.

"He hid it well. I think he wanted to show me and my mother that he didn't need anybody so he didn't talk to us about it or show any emotion. I thought he didn't care about her. But one day when I was older I saw him getting something down from a shelf in the garage, and one of Liz's old sweaters fell on him. He didn't know I was watching, otherwise I don't think he would've done it, but he sat down and held the sweater to his face and cried into it. This was years after her disappearance."

She nodded. "Jon, do you ever think about finding your sister?"

"Every day."

"But you have to realize that—"

"I know. But just knowing what happened to her would bring me a lot of peace."

Stanton felt a tug in his gut and emotion welled up inside

him. The full impact of what Oster had done dawned on him. Gunn would never catch Oster's partner. He was a narcotics detective who had transferred to homicide because it was more glamorous. All those families would feel exactly as Stanton felt just now.

"What is it?" she said.

"I just realized something." He stood up. "Unfortunately I'm gonna have to cut this session short, Jennifer. Please bill me for the full hour, though."

"I think we're having a good session. I'd like for you to stay."

"I'll come twice next week. But I have to do something right now."

He turned and walked out of the room, leaving her sitting there. She sighed, got up, went to her desk, and jotted the session's end time, making a note to bill him for the full hour.

CHAPTER 22

The first person Stanton called after he had left his therapist's office was Emma. She picked up on the third ring.

"Hey," she said.

"Emma, I have to break my promise to you. I have to see this case through."

"Why? I though—"

"I think I can stop him. I think two people committed these crimes and the other one is still out there. They have Stephen assigned to the case. He doesn't care about it. He'll close the case with Oster, and this other guy will get a pass for months, maybe even years until he screws up and gets arrested for something else. No one else can do this."

She was silent a long while.

"I'm sorry," he said.

"I can't keep going through this."

"I know." He paused. "Are you gonna answer later if I call?"

"Of course I'll answer. But I don't want to be near this. How about we just take off? Let's go to the Caribbean or Mexico. Right now. Today."

"I promise you when this case is closed I'll take you wherever you want to go in the world. They won't catch this guy without me, Emma. And all those families will have to live the rest of their lives with a glimmer of hope that their daughters and moms are still alive somewhere. That hope is what kills you. It leaves the wound open. You can't move on."

"Jon, I'm getting to the age where I want to settle down and have kids. I don't want my kids exposed to what you do. I don't want a husband that spends his time thinking about death all day. I won't have that."

"I know. I know. After this case, I think we should move."

"Move where?"

"Anywhere. We both have doctorates. I'm sure it won't be that difficult to get faculty positions in some small town in Montana or Arizona. They'll never leave me alone. Anytime they get stuck, they'll come to me."

"Why? I don't understand that. They have the whole damn police force to help them."

"These type of men are extremely rare. There're probably less than a hundred in the entire world hunting victims right now. The police force isn't set up to catch them. The FBI, with all their specialized training on serial murder and profilers and the most advanced databases and forensics, only has a thirty percent apprehension rate. Most of them get away. Danny and Kathleen are just looking for any edge they've got. But whenever something like this comes up, they'll want that edge again. They'll just keep coming back to me."

She was silent before saying, "I've got a great job. I don't know if I want to move."

"Can we just talk about it later? Don't decide anything right now. Let's just talk about it."

"All right, we'll talk about it."

"Okay. I...I love you."

"I love you too."

The words came so naturally, there wasn't that moment of awkwardness that usually accompanies saying them for the first time. Stanton hung up the phone before realizing he had missed his freeway entrance.

Stephen Gunn lived in a high rise similar to Stanton's but much more expensive. Stanton read the sign out front that said, LUXURY LIVING AT ITS FINEST. Stanton had seen policemen before, making no more than fifty or sixty thousand a year, living in half-a-million-dollar condos or driving hundred-thousand-dollar cars. Being on the take was nothing new, and Stanton had read enough police history to know it had existed since the first time someone put on a badge. But there was a difference between cops who stole a little off the top of a stack of cash taken from a drug dealer and the cops that actually dealt the drugs. Gunn, he was certain, fell into the latter category.

Stanton parked and had to be buzzed in. Gunn sounded like he had just woken up even though the sun was bright in the sky.

The elevator smelled like the perfume older women wear and big band music was playing in the background. Stanton stepped off on Gunn's floor and saw that his door was open. He walked in to Gunn on the patio in a bathrobe. Stanton glanced into the bedroom. A nude woman slept on the bed.

"The view's why I bought this place," Gunn said. "But it gets worse every day. You see that little grocer right there? Owner got stabbed in the face a few weeks ago. That little alley in between the apartment building and the restaurant is where some high-school kids come by every day after school and sell dope."

"You could call it in."

Gunn shook his head. "I won't do that. I'll walk over and bust their fuckin' heads open if they annoy me too much, but I won't call it in." He looked Stanton squarely in the face. "I ain't no snitch."

Stanton looked out over the streets. Stanton had testified against a former chief of police, Michael Harlow, in a corruption scandal years ago. Not a single uniform or detective—other than Childs who had seen the real extent of Harlow's fall from grace—had ever let Stanton forget it.

"Michael was my friend," Stanton said. "That was one of the most painful things I've ever had to do. But I had to do it. When he was in charge, there was no difference between us and them," Stanton said, motioning with his chin to the group of boys in the alley.

"It wasn't your place. It was IAD's."

"Harlow had IAD in his pocket. They never would've moved

on him."

Gunn shook his head. "Mike was the one who hired me when he was a sergeant. He saw something in me. I had no plans to be a cop. Mike talked me into it and said I could find a place there. Somewhere to fit in."

"I loved Mike more than you ever could, Stephen. But I don't regret what I did. And I didn't come here to talk about him."

"Why did you come here, Jon?"

"I'm gonna let Kathy know that I'm helping on this case. She needs me. And I wanted to tell you first."

He shook his head without looking at him. "That's a mistake. She doesn't need you. She's using you."

"Everyone in this system uses everyone else. If it's for a greater good, I can live with it."

Gunn walked inside and came back out with a lighter and a joint. He lit the joint and blew a puff of smoke toward Stanton, so he understood it wasn't a cigarette.

"She don't need you and I don't trust you."

"Why don't you trust me? Because you were going to kill Jaime and I wouldn't let you?"

"I wasn't gonna kill her. How fuckin' stupid do you think I am? I was just gonna scare her."

"How?"

He shrugged and took a puff off the joint. "Women need a reminder now and then of their place. Otherwise they'll ruin a man's life."

"I don't care about the past. I'm not a cop anymore and I'm never going to be. You do what you want. I just came to tell you that I'm going to be helping with this case."

He nodded, blowing out a thick cloud of smoke. "That's fine with me."

"I'm gonna go meet with some Vice detectives tonight and ask them about any porn actresses that have gone missing recently. I think it would help if someone with a badge was there with me."

Gunn looked to him. "Fine. Text me where you want to

meet." He turned back to the street below. "You know where the door is."

CHAPTER 23

Shaggy's Bar and Grill was near an old strip mall surrounded by motels and liquor stores. It was in an area known as Brickwood, which had once been a middle-class suburb for working families. But it had slowly degraded over time and the families had moved out and been replaced with junkies and prostitutes and alcoholics that were down on their luck.

Stanton was parked on the curb, watching the foot traffic. The prostitutes were huddled in groups on the corner and every once in a while he would see a car pull up, and one of the girls would climb in. After fifteen or twenty minutes, they would be dropped off again and take their place on the corner.

A man in jeans and a black T-shirt with greasy, unkempt hair walked on the sidewalk. He was glancing around like he was paranoid about someone following him before he walked into Shaggy's. Stanton looked in his rearview and saw Gunn sitting in his car. He waited a couple of minutes, nodded, and they got out and went inside.

Shaggy's was dark and smelled like marijuana smoke and alcohol. Detective George Springfield sat in the corner, nursing a beer. Gunn and Stanton sat down across from him.

"Well, well," Springfield said, "the prodigal son returns. What the fuck are you doing back with Homicide, Jon?"

"He don't take hints really well," Gunn said.

"I'm only meeting you because you said you're working this case with Stephen. If it was just you, you wouldn't be getting any help from me."

Stanton nodded. He understood even before he had testified

against another cop that this would be his punishment: no one would ever trust him again.

"So, I'm really busy. What do you want?"

"I was told you're working the adult film industry?" Stanton said.

"Me and two other guys. Why?"

"Just looking for underage girls in the films?"

"Pretty much."

"But you've built connections in the industry, right?"

"Yeah, all the directors and studio heads know us. They wanna be on our good side, so they work with us."

"Do you know the actors and actresses well?"

Springfield didn't answer. Stanton understood that, when they were assigned to this division, Vice cops sleeping with adult film stars was common. So common in fact, that many of the single detectives asked to be transferred to the unit.

"I don't care about any of that," Stanton said. "I want to know about any missing actresses in the past month. Have any just disappeared out of the blue?"

"You kidding me? Girls disappear all the time. Most of 'em are junkies and end up moving around or they become so burned out, they just end up under a bridge or on a corner somewhere. A lot of 'em get AIDS or hep and just leave and never come back."

"Can you think of any disappearance in the past month that was maybe unusual? Like the girl had some films or appointments lined up and she just never showed up?"

Springfield looked to Gunn, who slightly bowed his head as if giving him permission to talk.

"There was one. The boyfriend filed an MP report on her. He said some dude stuck a gun in his face and shoved her into a van and took off."

"What was her name?"

"Debbie Delicious. I think her real name was Natalie Heath."

CHAPTER 24

Stanton stepped out of the ocean and lay in the warm sand. It was still before 6:00 a.m. and the noise of families and tourists on the beach wasn't uncomfortable yet. He closed his eyes and let the warmth and the salty smell of the sea penetrate him for a long time before he got up and went home to shower and change.

Breakfast was egg whites on toast, and he grabbed a small bottle of orange juice before leaving the apartment. Once in the lobby, he saw the cleaning crew busy at work, vacuuming and dusting and polishing. He said hello in Spanish and chatted a few minutes with them about rumors going around the building. Apparently someone had tried to kill themselves on the fourth floor but had shot themselves with a low caliber pistol. Instead of killing themselves, the bullet lodged in their brain, blinding them. The conversation was making Stanton uncomfortable and he feigned being in a hurry and left.

San Diego Police Department Eastern Division was near a neighborhood Stanton knew well. It was called Allied Gardens. His ex-wife had moved nearby after the divorce. One thing that always surprised him was how many memories a massive city like San Diego could hold. He had thought that after the divorce there would be a slow healing process. His education in psychology told him there would be grieving and gradually he would accept the fact that she wasn't coming back, and the healing process would begin. But every time he drove by a restaurant they had enjoyed eating at or a television show came on that they had watched together, the wound was reopened and the healing process had to start over. His education hadn't told him that.

Stanton parked and went inside Eastern. No receptionist manned the large desk up front and he stood there for a few minutes until someone got up from another desk and came over.

"Can I help you?"

"I have an appointment with Detective Strand."

"Just a moment."

A few minutes after that, a large man in a wrinkled suit came out. He was holding a file under his arm.

"Jon," he said. "Good to see you."

"How are you, David?"

"Been better, been worse. How you been? I heard you're getting rich over there in the PI game."

"It's definitely better pay."

"Well what ain't?" He handed him the file. "What you asked for. I need it back by the end of the day or it's my ass."

"I was actually just going to read it here if that's okay."

"I'm glad you said that. I've been sweating it a little."

"You could've said no."

"You saved my ass more than once. I'm not saying no to you." He paused and glanced around. "Listen, I know you get a lotta shit for testifying against Harlow. But I think you did the right thing. That guy was too dangerous. He was giving us a bad rap. All of us."

"I appreciate that. I hate to ask for another favor but do you have somewhere quiet I can read for a few minutes?"

"Of course. Use my office. Come on, I'll show you where it is."

Stanton followed behind as they went to a small office around the corner. Several officers glared at him but said nothing.

The office was cramped and full of missing person files, the photos of the missing stapled to the outside of the folders. It was a trick Stanton had seen some of the most devoted MP detectives use. Having a photo to identify the victim instead of

a name made the case more personal and motivated the detective. Cases got worked harder, but it also caused the detectives
to take their work home with them. The faces would be etched
in their memories and many reported seeing the victims everywhere: at the grocery store or a restaurant or the ballpark. Stanton had used the same tactic with his murder files when he first
started but had abandoned the practice because, as his partner
at the time, Eli Sherman, had told him, "you're going to see dead
people everywhere."

"I'll leave you to it," Strand said before shutting the door.

Stanton sat down at the desk and placed the file in front of
him. The photo stapled to the front was of a beautiful young
girl smiling widely for the camera. Her lips were ruby red and
she wore just a little too much make-up, but her beauty came
through in a way that made Stanton pause and just stare at her.

He flipped open the file and read the biographical information sheet on the front flap:

NAME: Natalie Dallas Heath
DOB: 07/15/1992
OCCUPATION: Actress
EDUCATION: GED
GANG AFFILIATION: None
NEXT OF KIN: Rebecca Holly Neuman, Mother
AKA: Debbie Delicious, Natalie Rebecca Heath, Rebecca
Heath
TATTOOS: None

Stanton read through the rest of the biography. At the end
there was always a little space meant for the detective's notes.
Usually a place for them to write whether they thought it was a
legitimate kidnapping or a runaway. In the space a few scribbled
lines mentioned a boyfriend that had seen her be pushed into
a van. Other than the boyfriend's name, telephone number, and
place of employment, there was no information about him.

The rest of the file contained information gathered from

friends and relatives and a copy of Natalie's criminal history. She had several drug charges and two DUIs. Stanton flipped to the last page: the report was less than eight pages. It wouldn't be of any help to him.

He took out his phone and snapped a photo of the boyfriend's information. His name was Dillon and he worked as a cameraman for Depraved Film Productions. Stanton googled it and saw that it was based out of Los Angeles and specialized in fetish pornography, movies involving pregnant women or dwarfs or several other specializations. He put the address into Maps and left the office.

Strand was drinking coffee in the middle of the bullpen, which was nothing more than a grouping of cubicles, and shooting the breeze with a few officers.

"Thanks, David."

"You're welcome. You need anything else you call me."

"I will, thanks."

As he was leaving, Stanton heard one of the officers comment, "Why you helpin' that guy?"

The drive to North Hollywood was longer than Stanton remembered. And the fact that it was over ninety-eight degrees wasn't helping him concentrate. He played music from Moby on his iPod and rolled the windows down, letting the wind blow over him. The gnawing anxiety in his gut didn't go away.

North Hollywood was a diverse area that had been trying for years to renovate itself. It consisted primarily of middle-class working families but a spur of new start-ups had recently taken advantage of the cheap office space.

Stanton got off the Hollywood Freeway and followed Maps to a section of the neighborhood that had cookie-cutter, five- and six-story office buildings. He found the one he was looking for next to a movie theater complex.

As he stepped out of the car, his phone rang. It was a 531 number: the prefix for the San Diego Police. Stanton answered as he got out of the car and began walking toward the office building.

"This is Jon."

"Mr. Stanton, I'm glad I caught you. My name is Herman Ching. I'm with Internal Affairs. We've actually met once."

"Yeah, I remember." An image of Ching standing at the back of a room in a white suit and a blue tie while Stanton was grilled about Eli Sherman flashed in his mind. "What can I do for you?"

"I had a couple of questions about your partner if you've got some time."

"Which partner is that?"

"Stephen Gunn."

"He's not my partner."

"Oh, I...the information I received said you two were working the porn star cases together."

"I'm not working them. I'm consulting and only for a short period. Anything that has to do with Gunn, you can call him about."

"Has he ever mentioned a J.J. Oaks?" Ching said as if he hadn't heard Stanton. "J.J.'s in the hospital right now and had a few interesting things to say about Detective Gunn."

Stanton paused in front of the glass double doors. "You're gonna have to do your own work, Ching. Please don't call me again." Stanton hung up and went inside.

The atrium was large and had several offices on either side. A winding staircase led up to the other floors, and lining the walls were movie posters for films like, "Preggo Patty Does Harlem" and "Dirty Milfs."

No receptionist was around that he could see so he walked to the first office and poked his head in. A woman was busy on a computer, holding a pen between her lips. She glanced up at him.

"Yeah?" she said.

"I'm looking for Dillon Ashby."

"Upstairs second door on the left."

"Thanks."

Stanton used the elevator instead of the staircase and stepped off onto the second floor. He glanced down into one of the offices. A man with a camera filmed a nude woman that was on a couch. Another man stood by in a bathrobe, sipping a drink.

The second door on the left led into a studio. A bed, a couch, and a kitchen were set up with cameras and sound equipment everywhere. Several people filmed a shoot and two nude women, both massively obese, were receiving direction from a man in a baseball cap. Off to the side, Stanton could see a man receiving fellatio from a young woman. In the porn industry those girls were known as fluffers and their purpose was to keep the actors erect in between scenes. Many were hoping to break into porn and saw this as a first step, but Stanton had learned from Vice detectives long ago that the girls were seen as the lowest rung in porn. Abused and degraded, they were never given the big break they thought they were going to receive. Drug addiction and prostitution were typically their final stops.

The man in the baseball cap stepped away from the bed and checked the shot through the camera as another man in shorts readied the sound. The man in the cap noticed Stanton and said, "Who the hell are you?"

"I'm looking for Dillon Ashby," Stanton said.

"Dillon, some douchebag is here for you," the man shouted at the top of his lungs.

A young man in shorts came out. He had black circles under his eyes and Stanton could see the red and black track marks running up his arms. A cigarette dangled from his mouth and he placed sunglasses on.

"Yeah, I'm Dillon."

"My name's Jon Stanton. I'm a consultant with the San Diego Police Department. I have a few questions about Natalie if you've got a minute."

He took a drag of the cigarette. "Yeah, give me twenty minutes to shoot this scene and then we'll take a break."

Stanton glanced to the two women on the bed who had begun fondling each other. "I'll be outside."

Stanton walked around the second floor, peering into the office windows.

This was such an unusual world to him, he may as well have landed on a different planet. These people had grown so accustomed to sex it was seen as a commodity; giving it was nothing more than a bodily function, like urination. He couldn't imagine that they enjoyed it much. Though they probably told themselves they did.

One office held a studio filming a man being assaulted by several women in latex. One was filming two women rolling around nude on a wrestling mat. The last door on this level held just a desk and chair and Stanton went inside and sat down. He couldn't hear any groaning and realized the spaces had been soundproofed.

Playing on his phone for ten minutes, he stepped out and leaned against the railing another few minutes before Dillon came out and walked over to him.

"So, you a cop, huh?" he said nervously.

"No, I'm just a consultant."

"Oh, so you can't like arrest anybody then, huh?" he said, rubbing the back of his neck. Stanton could recognize the paranoia and jitteriness of someone in the middle of a meth binge. Their mood could change in an instant and they could become violent. He stepped away from the railing.

"Can you tell me about the night Natalie was taken?"

"We was just coming out of a place we ate at and this dude jumped out of a van and stuck a gun in my face. He just grabbed her and pulled her into the van and left."

"Did the detectives you spoke with after that ever have you sit down with a police sketch artist?"

"Yeah, but...I was pretty high. I didn't really remember enough. Medical marijuana, though. I got a license for it for anxiety."

"The van was black?"

"Yeah, black."

"Did it have California plates?"

"I don't remember. I think so."

"What type of gun was it?"

"I don't know, man."

"Did he say anything?"

"No."

"What kind of shoes was he wearing?" Stanton knew that while many were quick to discard clothing after a crime, they kept their shoes.

"I don't know."

"You told the detectives he was wearing a hat. What type of hat?"

"It was like a baseball hat."

"What team was it displaying?"

He thought a moment and then shook his head. "Sorry, man. I don't remember."

Stanton nodded, looking down to the floor below as several young women entered the building. "Dillon, I can tell you're pretty high right now. How many days have you been up?"

His eyes went wide. "I ain't high."

"I don't care. I told you, I'm not the police. But once you come down, I'd like you to visit someone with me."

"Who?"

"It's a hypnotherapist. I've used her a few times in situations like this. Your conscious mind was too impaired to have a vivid memory of anything, Dillon, but your unconscious is like a recording machine. The entire incident is locked away inside your mind. I would like you to spend just an hour with this woman. Her job is to bring that recording to the surface. I'll pay you for your time."

He thought about it. "All right. That's cool."

"But you need to be sober. When can you be sober?"

"I can do it in a couple days."

"All right. I'll come back here in a couple of days at lunchtime to pick you up. Is that all right?"

"Yeah, man, that's cool."

"Here's my card. If you think of anything or you need to reschedule, just call me."

"Okay. Cool."

As Stanton walked out of the building a young girl walked in. She seemed lost and glanced at him several times before asking, "Is this the studio?"

Stanton saw her high heels and the make-up that had been carefully applied. "There's nothing in there for you," he said. "They'll use you until you can't be used anymore and then you'll be thrown away."

"Who are you, my fucking dad?"

She brushed past him and went inside.

CHAPTER 25

As Stanton drove back to his apartment, his cell phone rang: it was his office. He answered and his secretary said that a Kyle Bonnie wanted to speak with him.

"Put him through." The line clicked and Stanton heard breathing. "What can I do for you, Kyle?"

"Oh, hi, Detective. I really hope I'm not bothering you."

"No bother. What's going on?"

"I just ah…I just was curious about how the investigation was going."

"It's progressing. Nothing substantive yet."

"Um, how did that interview with that sick fucker go?"

"It was fine, Kyle. We're doing everything we can right now."

"Oh, I know you are. I wasn't calling to check up on you. I'm just curious."

A long moment of silence before either of them spoke.

"Is there something specific you wanted to ask me?" Stanton said.

"No, I just wanted to see if the interview went well. I'll leave you alone now."

"I'm sure someone from the DA's Office will call you if there're any major updates."

"Okay. Thanks."

Stanton hung up but held the phone in his hand, tapping it lightly against his cheek. He held down a button and said, "Dial office." The iPhone called his office and the secretary picked up. "Kelly, run a background check on Kyle Bonnie. I don't have the middle name on me but if you call Daniel Childs at Northern, he can get that to you."

"Will do."

Stanton got home and changed into shorts and grabbed an orange juice before collapsing on his couch. He turned on the television, flipping through a few channels before turning it off and going out onto his balcony. He sat and put his feet up on the side table. The sun was still bright in the sky, and he could see people out on the waves. A game of volleyball was going on and he watched it. He kept his iPad next to him: a background report from the service he used only took about twenty minutes.

Before long, the iPad buzzed with a new email and Stanton opened it.

The report was detailed to a degree that would upset the general public if they knew how easy it was for others to get this information. Bills, financial records, large purchases, credit ratings, high-school transcripts, criminal histories, law suits, traffic tickets, and psychiatric information was all included.

The criminal history was a bit of a surprise: Kyle didn't have a single charge. Growing up in California, the majority of people had some minor charge on their histories, even if it was later expunged or sealed. But the bigger surprise was Kyle's financials. Stanton had expected to see immaculate financial records. Instead, they were filled with late payments, repossessions, and foreclosures. Kyle's credit score was pegged as extremely high risk.

Stanton leaned back and stared at the beach. How was it that an accountant could have such a messy financial history? As he began flipping through the report again someone knocked on his front door.

He answered. Stephen Gunn stood there sucking on a toothpick.

"How'd you get in?"

"Same way I always did: I wait for someone else. I ain't never liked buzzin' up to anywhere...so, can I come in?"

"Yeah, sure."

Gunn flopped onto the couch. "We got somethin'."

"What?"

"Raymond Valdez. You remember him?"

"Yeah, he was my prime suspect for Nina Blum's death."

"But you didn't have enough to move."

"No."

"You still think he's good for it?"

"He meets all the profile indicators. It wouldn't surprise me."

Gunn nodded. "Well, ol' Ray Ray is sittin' in County right now. He raped a jogger near Sunset Cliffs Park. Tried to strangle her too but she maced him and got away."

Stanton thought a moment. "That doesn't fit the pattern."

"You kiddin' me?"

"These guys stick to their patterns, Stephen. But if the opportunity presented itself and they thought they could get away with it, they might not be able to control themselves."

"That's what I've been saying." He stood up. "Let's go. I'll drive."

Every jail Stanton had ever been to was the same: dreary. They checked in and walked through security as Gunn flashed his badge. Raymond Valdez was in general population, waiting for his arraignment. He'd been pulled from lunch and sat in a small room used for family visits. It had a table and several chairs.

As soon as they entered the room and Raymond saw Stanton's face, he rolled his eyes.

"I thought I was done with you."

Stanton sat down across from him as Gunn leaned against the wall.

"We never did finish our interview," Stanton said.

"I told you all I had to say. I didn't kill that bitch and her family. I ain't messin' with no kids."

Gunn said, "No, you just kill young women."

"Yo I wasn't tryin' to kill her. I was tryin' to get her to be quiet. That's it, man. You can't hit me with no attempted murder."

Stanton said, "You'll serve almost as much time for the rape, Raymond."

"We got two witnesses," Gunn said. "Old couple walkin' by while you were rapin' her."

Stanton didn't flinch at the lie. Though the police had been allowed to lie to suspects ever since a Supreme Court case said they could in the sixties, Stanton had never really embraced it. Most criminals were career criminals and hung out in criminal circles. They spoke to each other. If one detective was seen as not keeping his word, it would get out, and suddenly interrogations would get much more difficult for that person.

"Raymond, you're going to do time for this," Stanton said. "What I want, though, is the reason. It's something I've been curious about since all those years ago. Why Nina Blum? She wasn't a porn star. She was a housewife. Why choose her?"

"You a stupid bastard, ain't you, esay?" He leaned forward. "I don't know who that bitch is. I ain't never seen her. I ain't never talked to her. I didn't kill no family."

"I need that information, Ray. I need to know where the other victims are buried. Help me find them and we'll help you. I'm not saying you're going to walk—we both know that will never happen. But maybe we can convince the FBI to take it and have the US Attorneys try you in federal court. Federal prison is a resort compared to state. You'd have classes. You could finish your—"

"I didn't fuckin' kill no porn stars!"

The two men looked at each other from across the table. Stanton nodded. "Okay, Ray. Then I'm sorry. I'm sorry I'm not going to be able to help you. You'll just have to take your chances with a jury."

Stanton rose and nodded to Gunn. The two men began to leave the room when Raymond yelled out, "Yo, hold on a sec."

Stanton turned to him.

"I can't give you that shit, man. I'm tellin' you, it wasn't me.

But I can give you somethin' else."

"What?"

"Children, man. Kids. Cartel's been bringin' 'em in from all over Mexico. They here, man. Workin' as hoes. I can give you who brought 'em in."

"Yeah, right," Gunn said. "You're gonna turn on the Cartel?"

"If the price is right, homie. Ain't no loyalty in this game no more. It's every man for himself."

Gunn looked to Stanton.

They left the room and stood in the corridor. A flyer on the wall behind Gunn announced a cleaning day for the jail.

"You think it's him?" Gunn said.

"I had him pegged for it from the beginning. His background fits. This new offense is unusual, but like I said, he may have just gotten to the point he can't control himself anymore."

"Well, I'm gonna get Child Abuse and Special Victims to follow up with him about the cartel thing. What do you wanna do with him?"

"Make him think we're offering a deal in exchange for the information. I need to do some follow-up. I've got nothing on him right now for the other killings. But it's possible we may have our guy."

CHAPTER 26

Stanton sat in his little office at the precinct. It was a Thursday afternoon and he had spent the entire day pinpointing the various victims' locations on a map of San Diego. He was staring at his computer screen now and the classic donut-shape came into view when he lighted up the locations on Google Maps.

Serial murderers, rapists, kidnappers, even burglars and muggers, fell into the donut shape. In an attempt to fool law enforcement, they wouldn't commit their crimes near their own homes. They would drive out to a different neighborhood, commit the crime, and then go back home. The next time, they would do the same thing but in a different area to make the crimes appear random and undetectable. Instead, they would create a foci in the middle where they lived.

Stanton looked at the area in the center of the circle on the map. That was where his killer lived. Right in the middle of La Jolla.

He attempted to log in to the police database and was amazed that his passwords hadn't been revoked. A red exclamation point in the corner told him that there was a problem with his authorization and that he should contact the administrator.

Stanton ran a check on all the black vans registered to owners that lived near the center of the circle. He came up with five hits. He printed off the list along with the owners' addresses and phone numbers. Then he pulled up a spreadsheet of all the victims with the dates of their disappearances, and began to call.

The first owner was a man in his seventies who had trouble hearing. He informed Stanton that his van was sitting on cinder blocks in the driveway and hadn't run since the eighties. Stanton made a note to drive by the house and check.

The next van was owned by a family who didn't answer when he called. The third was a company van for a landscaping and window washing company. When he called the fourth name on the list, Nate Duram, a young man answered.

"This is Nate."

"Nate, my name is Jon Stanton. I'm a consultant with the San Diego Police Department and I just have a couple of questions for you if you've got a minute."

"I'm actually really busy. Can you call back later?"

"It's pretty important. Tell you what, I'll just come by. Let me grab a couple of uniformed officers and we'll stop by your work. You still at Millar Construction?"

"No, man. I can't have cops showing up at my work."

"I just need five minutes."

"All right, hang on a sec…okay, what do you need?"

"Do you still own the black cargo van with license plate ending in 72?"

"Yeah."

Stanton glanced at the date of Nina Blum's death. "You had it six years ago too?"

"Yeah, I've had it about ten years."

He looked at the date Natalie Heath disappeared. "Where were you on July seventh?"

"Oh, um, what was that like two weeks ago? Um…what day was that?"

"A Friday."

"Oh, yeah. I was in Sacramento. My girl lives up there and I fly up every other weekend."

"I see. I'll just need some verification. If you can email me your ticket confirmation I'll follow up with the airline."

"Am I in trouble for something?"

"No, I'm just exploring all the options right now. A black van was spotted in a crime on that day."

"Oh. Well, I actually didn't have my van."

"Where was it?"

"I rented it out."

"To who?"

"Some dude. He said he just needed it for one night."

Stanton sped down the freeway with Hillel Slobavich in the passenger seat. The sketch artist was annoyed that he had been called away from his day job as a graphic designer, and was on his cell phone the entire drive. But the police department paid him ninety-five an hour and the drive was nearly an hour by itself.

They arrived at the construction site near a McDonald's in La Jolla. The parking lot was full with the dinner crowd. One of the construction workers, a man that appeared to be younger than thirty, saw them step out of the car and walked over.

"You Jon Stanton?"

"Yeah."

"Hey, I'm Nate. Thanks for not coming in a police car."

"No problem." He looked to Hillel. "This is our sketch artist. He'll be spending about twenty or thirty minutes with you. We can do it in the car or in the restaurant if you prefer."

"Inside's fine. I could use a burger anyway."

After ordering and sitting down, the sketch artist took out several comparison books and began setting up his pad. Stanton opened a note app and began writing.

"How do you know this man?" Stanton asked.

"I saw him here. He was eating and he saw me pull up and ran out and asked if he could rent my van the next day. He said he was moving and needed one, and the moving companies were all out. Said he'd pay me five hundred bucks if I let him take it."

"You weren't worried about him stealing it?"

"Said he'd leave his car with me as collateral. It was an Audi, way nice. I didn't drive it 'cause I was gone but it was easily worth ten times my shitty van."

"Had you ever seen him before?"

"No, man. First time was when he ran out of this place."

"What was his name?"

"I don't know. I think he said John."

"John what?"

"I don't know."

"You didn't look at identification at all?"

"Nope."

The sketch artist pushed his glasses farther up his nose. "You gave some stranger your van and didn't even ask his last name?"

"Hey, man, I got it back. What's the big deal? Five hundred bucks is what I make in a week."

Stanton leaned back in the chair. "Was there anything distinctive about him you remember?"

"Not really. Normal looking dude. Had a tattoo on his arm."

"What kind of tattoo?"

"It was like a bull. But it had like, a bodybuilder's body. Weird looking."

Stanton pulled up a painting of a Minotaur on his phone. "Is this it?"

"Yeah, not that exact one but something like that."

Stanton put the phone away. "I'm going to leave you with Hillel. He's going to take you through a drawing of the person that borrowed your van. As soon as he's done, he'll call me and I'll be back."

"Whoa, hold on a sec. I gotta work, man. I can't just be shootin' the shit with nerdalinger over here all day."

Stanton stood up and took out his wallet. "A hundred bucks for half an hour of your time. That should be enough, right?"

"It's getting there."

Stanton took out another fifty.

"Almost there," Nate said.

"You know what, forget it. I'll just get a uniform down here to arrest you and bring you in for questioning and we'll do it there."

"Arrest me for what?"

"Accomplice to murder," Stanton said, taking his phone back out and pretending to dial a number.

"Whoa, whoa, it's cool, man. One fifty is cool. I'm all right."

"Be as accurate as possible. This man is very dangerous and the sooner you help us find him the sooner you'll be safe."

"Me? What did I do?"

"You've seen his face. You might be the only link we have to him. As soon as he realizes that, he might come looking for you."

Nate swallowed. "Um, should I be worried?"

"Just be accurate and take your time. If you need me to talk to your boss I will."

"Nah, he's cool. So what'd this guy do?"

"You don't want to know."

CHAPTER 27

The ocean waves lapped gently against the shore. It was well past midnight and there was no moon in the cloudless sky.

Stanton sat in the sand. He had fallen asleep at around ten and then woken up an hour later with a massive migraine. After Advil and a Diet Coke, he walked to the beach and sat down, staring out over the water. He had brought his phone, and as the migraine faded, he took it out and began researching the Minotaur.

The Minotaur was popularized in the myth of Theseus. Minos, the king, had ordered the people of Athens to provide a sacrifice every year. Seven young men and unmarried women would be sent to Crete and they would then be placed in the dark, damp, labyrinth with the Minotaur at its center.

Popularized myth told how the Minotaur would kill and eat the youths, but the original myth was far darker. The Minotaur only had the head of a bull; its body was of a giant man. He was portrayed as a sexual being with male sexual organs. The youths were not just killed and eaten, they were raped. Often for long periods of time as the Minotaur was said to have enormous stamina. When he was satisfied sexually, the sacrifices would be butchered and eaten.

The myth said that the Athenian hero Theseus had defeated the Minotaur by using a sword given to him by the daughter of King Minos. He came upon the sleeping Minotaur, who was surrounded with skeletal remains and decaying, ravaged corpses. The Minotaur awoke and they fought, Theseus defeating it only by stabbing it through the throat.

An image flashed in Stanton's mind: a home basement. A young girl locked away in chains, nude and bleeding. A monster sleeping nearby so he could listen to her cry at night. It was a dungeon not unlike the center of the labyrinth. He kept the girls, presumably, for a long period of time. He would need somewhere private to do so.

Stanton's cell phone buzzed: it was his ex-wife.

"Hey, Mel."

"Hey, hope I didn't wake you."

"No I was up. But isn't it like two in the morning over there?"

"No, we're not on the coast. We're in Maui right now. We've been scuba diving all day. Matt's really got the hang of it."

"That's great. I didn't realize you were out there."

"Just kind of a last-minute thing." She paused. "How are you doing?"

"I'm fine. Why?"

"I just thought...because of today and all."

Stanton wondered if he had missed a birthday or some other occasion, but July twenty-first didn't hold any meaning for him.

"What's today?"

"You don't remember?"

"Should I?" he said.

"It's the day you got shot, Jon."

A rush of memories flooded his mind. July 21, 2008. That was the date Eli Sherman had put two slugs in him and sent him to the hospital for over a month. Stanton glanced down to the scar on his chest coming up about two inches above his shirt.

"I hadn't thought about it in a long time," he said.

"Are they any closer to catching him?"

"No, I don't think so. After his escape he got out on a fake passport and bounced around South America for a while. I think the FBI was about a week too late in Rio where he'd been staying. There haven't been any sightings since."

"He's like Elvis. People are seeing him everywhere."

"I don't think anyone outside of San Diego cares who he is." Stanton took off his shoes and buried his feet in the warm sand.

"Are you ever scared, Jon?"

"That he might come after me? No. I don't think he would. I have no idea how I know that, but I just do."

"I think about him sometimes. How I used to cook for you two. He would sit at the table and compliment my food and I thought how lucky you were to have a nice partner for once."

"He fooled a lot of people. It doesn't say anything about you that you couldn't see it."

"The same applies to you, you know. You beat yourself up about this more than you need to." Stanton heard a male's voice in the background asking who was on the line. "I better go, Jon. I just wanted to check on you."

"I appreciate that. Thanks."

Stanton hung up and exhaled. He leaned back on the sand and stared at the black sky with its pinholes of light. He wondered if there really was anybody up there staring back down at him.

CHAPTER 28

Stanton woke at high tide when the cool water licked his feet. He sat up and looked over a pink sky as several surfers ran past him and into the ocean. He watched them a while before standing and heading back to his apartment. His cell phone had several messages from his office about clients that wanted to speak with him. He skipped those and went to the last message, something from Kathleen.

Jon, call me right away.

Stanton called her back as he walked across the beach.

"This is Kathy."

"Hey, it's Jon."

"Oh, hey. Danny's been trying to find you."

"What's up?"

"You know that girl you've been looking into, Natalie Heath?"

Stanton's heart sank. "Yeah."

"They found her body."

The neighborhood was upscale and clean, away from the traffic of busy intersections and freeways. As Stanton stepped out of his car, he was struck by how much quieter affluent neighborhoods were.

Police tape barricaded the front door of the home and several cruisers and the ME's van were parked on the curb. Stanton walked up to the door and a uniform stopped him.

"Closed scene."

"I'm a consultant. Lieutenant Childs is expecting me."

"Let him through," Childs yelled from somewhere inside.

Stanton ducked underneath the police tape and walked past several officers that didn't make way for him.

"Excuse me," he said.

He got to the kitchen and saw one of the forensic techs filming in the bedroom just down the hall. He walked over to him and stepped inside the bedroom.

Blood covered the carpet and the tech looked at him like he was crazy. He stepped back outside so as not to contaminate anything and just peeked into the room from around the corner until the tech brought out booties, a hair net, and latex gloves for him.

Natalie Heath lay nude and spread eagle on the bed. Her head had been sawed off her torso and blood had soaked the bed a dark black. Her breasts had been removed and bite marks covered her skin, which had turned an ashen gray, indicating that she had bled out before death. The head lay on a pillow and her eyes were open, staring helplessly at the ceiling.

"One of the officers ran outside and threw up," the tech said. "This is definitely one of the worst I've seen." He said it in an almost gleeful way that made Stanton look at him. The tech cleared his throat. "No sign of forced entry anywhere. Either the door was open or he had a key."

Gunn walked into the room behind Stanton. "Holy shit."

Stanton ignored him and approached the bed. The girl had been scalped, but the tangle of bloody flesh and hair had been placed back on her head. He leaned in closer and saw that it had been stapled back on with thick, metal staples.

"You know what this reminds me of?" Gunn said. "That fucker from last year. Stark."

"This is worse than Nina Blum. The killer's evolving. He's torn her completely apart. Look at the wounds on the legs. He tried to cut them off but stopped."

"Why would he stop?"

A single, terrifying image of a beautiful girl in a dark, damp basement came to his mind. "She probably died before he was through with her. She's decapitated but I bet that was postmortem. She would've passed out from the shock within a few seconds and he wouldn't have wanted that. He would've wanted to watch her suffering."

Gunn shook his head. "We're worse than animals."

Animals. That's what Stanton had thought of when he first came into the room. He had studied leopard attacks in Africa on a safari there. One leopard had been terrorizing the village they had been staying at and Stanton had seen what a hundred-and-fifty-pound animal could do to a human being.

"He thinks he's a Minotaur," Stanton said.

"What?"

"The tattoo. He thinks he's a Minotaur. Look at how deep the bite marks are. Most of them took away flesh, which he probably ate."

The tech chimed in and said, "Eww."

After both of them looked up at him, he cleared his throat again and said, "I'll just be in the hall until you guys are done."

"This was a frenzy attack," Stanton said to the tech. "Which means he wasn't careful about hair fibers or semen. Run his DNA through ViCAP and let me know right away if you get a hit. Childs has my cell phone number."

"Yessir," he said sarcastically. "Oh, wait, you're not my boss."

"But I am," Gunn said, "and unless you want me to fuck you with that camera before I fire your ass, you better get the hell outta here and do what he said."

The tech scowled and mumbled under his breath before leaving.

"Fucking show," Gunn said. "These *CSI* nerds think they run the circus."

"He's getting more brutal," Stanton said, looking at the body.

"So since Valdez is in custody he's not your man, huh?"

"Guess not."

CHAPTER 29

Stanton picked up Gunn early the next morning. Gunn got into the car, reeking of booze and sex. He pulled out a cigarette and lit it, opening the passenger window as they pulled away. Gunn noticed the small Book of Mormon on the center console.

"That for me?" he said.

"I just read some passages here and there at stoplights."

Gunn shook his head. "You're from another century, man. Science killed religion a long time ago."

"You would actually like this book."

"Get outta here."

"No, I'm serious. A lot of it chronicles wars and battles. That seems right up your alley."

"I'll pass. I like my coffee. So who we meeting with?"

Stanton turned onto the freeway entrance. "Her name's Nadia Felix. She's a casting director for adult films. I want to see if she can remember anyone on cast or crew that has a Minotaur tattoo."

Gunn let out a long puff of smoke. Stanton got the faint whiff of marijuana. "You know," Gunn said, "I dated a porn star once."

"Really?"

"Yeah, didn't last, though. She was a junkie. Tell you, though, man. That girl taught me some things."

Within an hour they were parking at a Starbucks near a shopping mall. The interior was crowded and several people sat alone at the tables. Gunn ordered coffee and tried to get Stanton to have one too, but he just asked for a milk steamer.

A woman in a business suit sat by herself at a corner table, flipping through a Blackberry. Stanton approached her, and she looked up, revealing deep blue eyes.

"Are you Nadia?"

"Yes, Jon? Nice to meet you."

"You too." He glanced over to Gunn, who had struck up a conversation with the barista and was leaning on the counter, flirting with her.

"I always find it funny when you need our help," she said.

"What do you mean?"

"The police, the FBI sometimes. Help with runaways and things. When we need you guys, you're never there for us. Porn is the most stolen entity on earth. You can't enforce your copyrights and trademarks on it, and people post it on the internet all the time. Where's the outrage over that? The music and movie industries get protection, but because you don't agree with what we're doing, we don't get any? The hypocrisy just gets to me sometimes. I thought it was equal treatment under the law."

"There's always been prosecutorial discretion. Adultery is still a crime on the books but no one enforces it." Stanton sat across from her and she put her Blackberry down.

"This isn't two people having sex behind closed doors. We're talking about millions of dollars stolen from us and the government sits back and says 'too bad.' That hardly strikes me as justice."

"Have candidates run for office and try to change it. I'm not a cop and I'm not here to argue politics, Nadia. I want to find the person killing your girls."

She stared at him a moment. "I couldn't find much. There's no database of tattoos. I checked with the Adult Entertainment Actor's Guild, but they didn't have anything. So I asked around, talked with some of the more popular directors. No one remembers anyone with a tattoo of a Minotaur on their arm. Sorry."

Stanton leaned back. "You could've texted me that. But you kept the meeting. Was there something you wanted to tell me in person?"

She glanced out the window. When she looked back, tears were forming. "Natalie Heath...she and I were...we were together."

"Natalie had a boyfriend."

"Of course. Everyone in this town has an extra boyfriend or girlfriend. That's how it is."

"Is there anything you can tell me?"

"The night she disappeared...I talked to her that night. She was going to dump Dillon."

"Why?"

"He'd been pressuring her to tell her family that they were getting engaged. Her family hated Dillon. He'd show up high to their family gatherings, hit on her sister, stuff like that. Natalie's dad asked him to leave their house once. So she was going to break it off with him."

"You think Dillon might be responsible for this?"

"I don't know. He has a temper. A bad one. He hurt a girl once on a set. She was dating him and during a gangbang scene, he just got really jealous and grabbed her by the hair and pulled her off set. She got a restraining order against him a little after that."

"Other than Dillon, was there anybody in Natalie's life that she was worried about?"

"Not really, no. She would just tell me about Dillon. She said he couldn't get off unless there was violence. He would need to hit her or choke her."

"Strangle."

"Excuse me?"

"Choke is internal, strangle is external. Is there anything else you can tell me?"

"No, that's it. Just that I wouldn't be surprised if Dillon killed her after she told him she was dumping him."

"I appreciate that, Nadia. I'll look into him a little more closely."

She nodded. "Do you need anything else?"

Stanton leaned forward on his elbows. "I've heard that a lot of these girls develop substance abuse problems."

"Junkies, you mean? You don't need to be PC with me. Yes, a lot of the girls are junkies."

"Do they have a common dealer? Someone popular that maybe served the victims?"

"Hm. Yeah, it's possible. They have dealers come on set. Like they're just delivering a pizza or something. I'll ask around and see who the regulars are."

Stanton stood up, glancing over to Gunn, who had just gotten the girl's number and was walking over. "I appreciate your time, Nadia. I'm sorry about Natalie."

"Me too."

CHAPTER 30

Stanton sat outside in the car as Detective Stephen Gunn entered the dance club. This particular dance club had been cited an average of ten times per year for violations until, according to Gunn, they had struck a deal with the Vice detectives and were now paying them off. With money and drugs and occasionally women.

Stanton checked his phone: it had been half an hour. Gunn had said he would be out in ten minutes tops.

He opened the door and walked to the club's entrance. A full moon hung in the sky like a white ball about to plummet to the earth. The air was warm. Stanton was still in his suit and he turned around and placed his coat in the car before walking inside.

He paid the bouncer the twenty dollar admission fee since he didn't have a badge any longer and went inside.

A mass of flesh was crammed onto the dance floor. The girls wore skimpy skirts and dresses or tight shorts that hugged their backsides and exposed their legs. The men were more varied and Stanton could see emos, glams, gays, punks, and gangsters all dancing together. Although a youthful energy exuded from the club, it was a violent, uncontrollable energy. Like a powder keg with a lit fuse. At any moment, any one of these kids could potentially pull out a weapon and hurt a lot of people.

Stanton looked for Gunn but didn't see him on the floor. He walked to the other side of the club, slipping past the youths who gave him curious stares. One girl, with a torn shirt exposing part of her breast, began dancing in front of him, rubbing herself against him. He gently brushed past her and approached the bar on the other side.

The bar was more mellow but just as dangerous. Everyone here was nearly catatonic. Clearly the club didn't limit how much booze it served its patrons.

Gunn wasn't in here either, but before Stanton turned to leave, he saw a set of stairs leading to a second floor. He took them and came upon several tables and couches and a few beds up against the far wall. Gunn sat with several men and a few women at a table, taking shots. Lines of cocaine were spread on the table like food, and one of the men or women would casually take a snort before getting back into the conversation.

Gunn saw him and motioned for him to come over.

Stanton recognized several of the men. They were part of the Vice squad and had become fixtures there. The official policy called for the rotation of detectives every two years to keep corruption at bay. A policy instituted after the fall of Police Chief Michael Harlow and the resulting federal corruption and racketeering charges throughout the department.

But the Vice detectives could apply for exceptions, claiming they had developed contacts that would be lost if they were transferred out. Though that had a veneer of plausibility, Stanton knew the real reason they stayed was that they had become addicted—either to drugs, sex, or power—and nothing was going to make them give that up.

"You guys remember Jon," Gunn yelled.

A bald man with a handlebar mustache smiled and let out a puff of smoke. "Jon Stanton. I thought you died."

"Rumors of my death were greatly exaggerated."

The man chuckled and took a straw, sucking up a line of coke and then putting his finger to his other nostril and snorting. Stanton could tell he did it just to show him that he could.

"Still chasin' after bedwetters, huh? Heard one hacked up some whore pretty good yesterday."

Because bedwetting is part of the serial murder triumvirate, the homicide detectives had come to calling the perps "bedwetters" to distinguish them from those who killed for money or revenge. Though it was a mechanism to cope with the horror of what they saw, Stanton thought it trivialized the suffering those individuals had brought into the world, and never liked the term.

"I see you're still snorting your paycheck up your nose. Has your wife left you yet?" Stanton had seen the lack of a wedding ring on his finger. He knew that he always wore his ring, no exceptions. Even undercover. Part of it was practical: if the mark they were undercover for saw the tan line or indentation they might get suspicious. Much better to just admit to marriage.

The man shot up in his chair. Rage filled his eyes. He grabbed a beer bottle off the table and hurled it at Stanton's head. Stanton ducked, just barely missing it, as the man tried to jump over the table at him. Several men grabbed him, holding him back as he spewed profanities. Gunn laughed, took a shot of something on the table, and stood up.

"Well," Gunn said, "we've overstayed our welcome. Take it easy, guys."

Neither of them spoke until they got outside.

"Man," Gunn said, "you go for the jugular, don't you?"

Stanton had always had an ability to hone in on a person's softest spots emotionally. When he lost his temper, he could devastate people with a few words, but it was rarely intentional. "I feel terrible I said that. I have to go apologize."

Gunn grabbed him. "What's done is done. Besides, you didn't say anythin' that wasn't true. His wife ran off with some lawyer. It happens."

They climbed into the car and Gunn pulled away from the club.

"Did you get a list?" Stanton said.

"Yup." Gunn fished out a scrap of paper from his pocket. "These are the best tattoo shops in the city. These four give ninety percent of the tattoos. If our boy got his bull tattoo here, he probably went to one of these four places—and we're one step closer to catching the bastard."

CHAPTER 31

After a quick meal of sandwiches at a local café, Stanton and Gunn went to the first tattoo shop on the list. It was in an upscale business district in North County next to a massage parlor and a French restaurant. They sat parked outside until Gunn had finished a cigarette and then went in.

Several workstations were set up around the space, and the walls were exposed brick. Leather furniture was spread throughout. A woman had her top off as an Asian man worked on a tattoo of a butterfly that covered the expanse of her back.

"Excuse me," Stanton said, "I'd like to speak with the owner or manager please."

"Upstairs," the man said without looking up, "I'll get him when I'm done."

"We're in a little bit of a hurry. It won't take more than ten minutes."

He stopped his needle and turned to them. "I said I would get him when I'm done. Now sit your asses down or get the fuck outta here."

He went back to work and before Stanton could get out another word, Gunn had dashed over and ripped the tattoo needle out of the man's hand. He swung it down like a knife into the man's forearm.

The tattooer screamed and began to fight but Gunn was on top of him. He kicked out one of the man's knees, forcing him down as the woman screamed and leapt off the table. Gunn was about to bash his fist into the guy's face when Stanton locked him in a half-nelson and pulled him back.

"Get the fuck off me!" Gunn shouted. He spun and knocked Stanton back.

Gunn stood over the tattoo artist, brass knuckles wrapped around his right hand, drool beginning to slink down over his lips.

"Hey!" The manager stood at the top of a staircase, wearing all black. He stomped down. "What the fuck is going on here?"

Gunn showed him the tin. "You're gonna be helping us a little."

The manager helped the artist up and went outside to see if he could find the patron, but she was gone.

"You guys in the habit of ruining small businesses?" he said when he came back.

"Help us and you'll never see us again," Gunn said.

The manager nodded. "What do you need?"

The manager took Gunn to the books after telling his employee to take the night off and go to the hospital.

The tattoo books contained snapshots of all the tattoos that had been given at the shop. Stanton sat down with an armful on a couch and Gunn did the same. Going through them in silence, they didn't realize until half an hour later that the books were organized by theme. They went through the pages under mythology, animals, mysticism, and religion, but didn't see a Minotaur.

"Thank you for your help," Stanton said as they left. The manager nodded but didn't say anything.

When they were outside, Stanton stood in front of the car as Gunn pulled out a package of cigarettes. When he lit one, Stanton stared at him.

"What?" Gunn said.

"You know what."

"That's the problem with you, Johnny. You were never able to crack heads when you needed to."

"You could've showed him your badge and he probably would've gotten his manager. There was no need to send him to the hospital."

"These fuckers out here don't respect the badge, you kiddin' me?"

"But you didn't even try. You just hurt him the second he didn't do what you wanted."

"So what?"

"So why do you do it? I want to understand. Why do you prefer violence when words will suffice?"

He looked at Stanton calmly as he took a drag from his cigarette and leaned against the car. "That's what we are."

"Who? Cops?"

"No, people, man. We're killers. Some of us fight it and some of us embrace it. Nehor Stark, as sick as that bastard was, he understood. He embraced it. He wanted to burn buildings with people inside and he did it. He did it 'cause it brought him pleasure."

"That's the fantasy, Stephen. All these people, Oster, Sherman, Stark, they all think it's going to bring them pleasure, but it doesn't. They have a hole in the middle of their souls and they think imposing suffering will fill it. That's why they have to keep killing. Just like a heroin addict who can never get a good fix after the first one. But they'll keep chasing that first fix, hoping that the next one will be just like it. It never is. Stabbing that innocent man in the arm didn't bring you pleasure. It had nothing to do with pleasure."

He shrugged and threw the cigarette on the ground, stepping on it. "Maybe it did and maybe it didn't. You ready?"

Stanton was silent. "Sure, I'm ready."

The second tattoo shop was more helpful. Several of their staff brought out books and helped Stanton and Gunn go through them. The third was closed and had a sign that said the closure was indefinite.

The next one on the list was in Escondido. It was a small shop called Shank's with just two workstations and a clean black floor. They didn't arrive until nearly eleven but the shop

VICTOR METHOS

was open and the owner, a huge biker type whom the shop was named after, was giving a young man a tattoo on his penis. It was the name of a girl.

Gunn said, "You know as soon as that heals she's gonna break up with you, right? I think your future wife may have a problem with that."

"I ain't never getting married."

Gunn shrugged. "Suit yourself."

Shank stopped the needle and put antiseptic and a clear plastic bandage over the tattoo. After the young man paid, Shank followed him out and turned off the OPEN sign.

"What can I do you for, Officers?"

"We're looking for a man that received a specific tattoo. A Minotaur, on either his left or right forearm."

"Hm. Hang on a sec." He went behind the counter and pulled up a file on the computer. He kept all his photos digitally, and it only took him a moment to type in MINOTAUR and come up with two hits. One was a tattoo on a calf, the other on a forearm.

Stanton looked at the one on the forearm. The Minotaur was muscular and stood over several body parts, blood dripping down its bare chest. In his right hand was the severed head of a woman.

"Who got that tattoo?"

"I don't keep names, brother. Sorry. But he got this on December 13 in '04. If he paid with a credit card, maybe you can track it down."

"Do you remember anything about him?"

He shook his head. "Long time ago and my memory ain't what it used to be. I ain't a young man anymore."

"Can you please print that off for me?"

"Sure."

Shank printed out a color copy and Stanton brought it over to Gunn, who was sitting nearby in the waiting area.

"That's gotta be him, right?"

"I don't know. I'll follow up with the major credit card companies and see if anyone has a purchase here on this date."

156

Gunn nodded. "Good. Let's get outta here. I got a piece a ass waitin' for me."

CHAPTER 32

Stanton sat in his office at the precinct and called one credit card company after another. He figured out that he was on hold an average of twenty-three minutes with each one before speaking with someone that could answer his question. The answer was always the same: "I dunno know. That was a long time ago."

Visa, MasterCard, and Discover didn't show any purchases at Shank's. He tried a few lesser-known cards and then American Express. Not a single one had a record of a purchase on that date at that tattoo parlor. But several of them said the record for an account that had been closed might not be kept for that far back.

A knock at the door and he looked up to see Emma standing there, a white bag and two soft drinks in her hands.

"Hey," she said.

"Hey. Come in."

She sat and glanced around the office. "No decorations?"

"I didn't want to be here this long."

"Why don't you work out of your own office?"

"I want to keep these two worlds separate. What're you doing up here?"

"Just wanted to bring you lunch. Philly cheesesteaks and Diet Cokes."

Stanton reached into the bag and brought out a sandwich wrapped in butcher paper. "I love these, thanks."

"So how's everything going?"

"It's going." He took a bite and the cheese was so gooey it dribbled down his chin. He wiped at it with a napkin. "What're you doing here, Emma? I thought you hated police precincts?"

"I do. I just miss you."

"I haven't been the best boyfriend lately."

"No, it's fine. It really is. I get it. I'm just not used to seeing you so little."

Stanton, suddenly and for the first time, could see exactly why his marriage had fallen apart. It had nothing to do with changing personalities or growing apart or the nature of his work. He simply was not there enough for his wife and she was lonely. Unexpectedly, he felt pity for her for having to be so alone for so many years.

"Jon, you still with me?"

"Yeah, sorry. I was just thinking about something."

"I can go if you—"

"No, please stay. I really needed to see you just now."

She smiled and pulled out her sandwich.

They ate and talked about the latest goings-on at UCLA. Emma had been invited to be a guest lecturer on organic electronics. Though it was just a side project she'd been working on the past few years, she had made tremendous strides in improving LEDs, and Harvard had asked if she would be there as part of a symposium.

"Are you going to go?"

"Yeah, I think I am."

"How long will you be gone for?"

"A week. The symposium's four days and I'm going to spend some time with my sister after that. Come with me. You need a vacation from all this."

"I can't."

"I don't see any handcuffs on you. Nobody's holding a gun to your head. What you mean to say is that you won't."

"I'm close, Emma. I can...*feel* him. I don't know how else to describe it. No one else can do this."

She nodded. "Of all the things to be good at in the world, why'd you have to pick this one?"

"I didn't pick anything. It picked me."

VICTOR METHOS

She pushed aside the rest of her sandwich and walked around the desk, sitting on his lap. Kissing him, she put her arms around him. They held each other a long time before she got up, cleaned up the sandwiches, and said she would call him when she got to Boston.

"Can I at least drive you to the airport?" he asked.

"Sure. The flight's at seven tomorrow morning."

"I'll pick you up at five."

A final kiss and Stanton watched her walk out of the office. He looked down to the files stacked neatly on the desk but couldn't bring himself to open them.

"You okay?"

He looked up to see Daniel Childs in the hallway.

"Yeah, fine, Danny. Thanks."

"That's a hot little woman you got there," he said, coming near the door but not through it.

"Yeah, she's great. And I just let her go to Boston for a week without me so I could stay here and look through these files. What the hell's wrong with me, Danny?"

"You ain't the problem, man. Files like that shouldn't exist in the first place."

CHAPTER 33

By 7:00 p.m., Stanton had concluded that the credit card companies were absolutely no help. People complained about the inefficiency of government but every time he'd gone to the DMV he'd gotten what he'd needed quickly and without much fuss. Dealing with the mega-corporations had always been more difficult. It was as if people there didn't know what the others were doing or saying and nothing would get done.

He leaned back in the chair and looked at the printout of the Minotaur tattoo, which he'd laminated. Though it was just a drawing, the sheer barbarism of it was difficult to look at. The expression on the countenance of the severed head was one of absolute terror, utterly and completely. Something Stanton had seen on the faces of several victims.

Hold on, just hold on. I'm coming for you.

He stood up and headed out of the precinct with the print-out in hand.

Stanton waited nearly forty minutes before Philip Oster was brought out. It had taken the prison staff that long to search him, cuff him, and walk him down. He was sat in front of Stanton and had a grin on his face.

"It's different bein' in here when it's dark, ain't it?" Oster said.

"I don't think it's ever pleasant being in here."

"Ain't that the truth. But as lock-ups go, this ain't a bad one. I'm earnin' my associate's degree in mechanical engineering in here through the community college. Don't know why since they ain't never gonna let me out, but a man's gotta keep his mind occupied."

Stanton slid the piece of laminated paper across the metal desk. Oster looked at it and smiled.

"Did you find him?"

"No. But now I know I'm on the right track."

"I didn't say that."

"You didn't have to."

He seemed to relax and leaned back in his seat, playing absent-mindedly with the cuffs on his wrists. "Your DA friend came back here. She gave my attorney a contract. I told her to shove it up her cunt. I don't think she liked that much."

"So you're not confessing?"

"No, I really didn't want a deal. See them families out there'll make enough of a stink once they find out I know where their little girls are buried. I'll let them do the fightin' for me."

"They'll never let you out of this place, Philip. No matter how many bodies you give them."

"I don't need to get out. I ain't really got anythin' out there anyway. I want a transfer to minimum security. I want satellite TV and to hang out with white-collar guys. Dudes that stole from companies. I'm sick a hanging out with these dope fiends and child molester bastards."

Stanton watched him. It was an interesting compartmentalization he'd seen before. Even the most grotesque rapists and serial murderers looked down on someone, usually child molesters. A coping mechanism that in their minds gave them some sort of rudimentary morality. Even Eli Sherman had been disgusted with child sex cases.

"Help me find him."

"No way, brother. He's my ticket outta here."

"Not if he keeps killing and you're holding out. Did you know we found the body of another girl? Semen was found in the anal cavity. Didn't match anything we or the FBI have on file."

"No, he ain't never been in trouble before. You ain't gonna

find him that way."

"Why Jill Bonnie? Why'd he choose her first?"

It only lasted a moment, but a slight furrow of Oster's brow told Stanton exactly what he needed to know.

"She wasn't the first," Stanton said. "She was *your* first, wasn't she?"

"No."

"You're lying. The pattern changed with Nina Blum. That's when the killings became bloody and violent. Nina Blum was his first, wasn't she?"

"No," he said, frustrated.

"You're lying again."

"You don't know shit about me. Quit sayin' that."

"I know everything about you. I know why you did what you did."

"Oh yeah? Learn me somethin' then."

"You did it because you think that's how you can achieve absolute pleasure. A willing sexual partner thinks about their own pleasure too. That means they're not completely focused on you. You think an unwilling partner is the only way to get the attention completely on you and have them focus on nothing else. If you want absolute pleasure, you have to have absolute power."

He smirked. "I had a feelin' me and you were the same."

"We're not the same. I said you think that's the way to absolute pleasure but you're wrong. Each girl brings you less pleasure than the last and you don't understand why. You've focused in on a symptom and left your disease untreated."

"Yeah? And what's my disease?"

"You hate yourself. You really want to kill yourself, but you're too scared of death to do it. Every one of these attacks was an attack on yourself."

He shook his head. "You're so full of shit. I read up about you, *Detective*. You got the most kills in the PDs history. You think you're any better than me? You ain't shit."

Stanton took the printout and stood up. "Thank you for

this, Philip. You've given me everything I needed."

"Hey fuck you!" he shouted, jumping to his feet. In a moment the guard was on him and pulling his arms up behind his back for control. "Hey, I hope you do find the motherfucker and he kills you! He ain't as nice as I am. You hear me, Detective? He ain't as nice."

CHAPTER 34

After dropping Emma off at the airport the next morning, Stanton headed directly to the Pepsi distribution warehouse where Nina Blum's brother worked as a shipping clerk. It was in an industrial part of the city far away from the beach. The farther Stanton got from the water, the more disconnected and out of sorts with himself he felt. He wondered if that sort of connection to nature was healthy. The ancient Native Americans certainly believed it was and there had been a tribe, the Anasazi, not far from San Diego that worshipped the ocean. They believed it was the great mother that provided all they needed to live and that if you had a connection to the ocean, everything else was unnecessary.

Stanton arrived at the distribution outlet fifteen minutes before they opened and sat in his car, listening to a Depeche Mode album. When the distribution center opened, he went inside and found the secretary booting up her computer.

"Dennis Ramell, please," he said.

A few minutes later a pudgy man in a zip-up work uniform stepped out. Stanton remembered him from the first investigation years ago. Dennis had now gained at least thirty pounds and his hair was gray where before it had been a dark black. His hands and nails were black with grime and oil.

"What can I do for you?"

"You don't remember me, Mr. Ramell? I investigated the death of your sister about six years ago."

"Oh. Well I remember talkin' to some cops but I don't remember who. Let's walk outside."

VICTOR METHOS

Stanton followed him out the door and into the parking lot.

"Sorry," Dennis said, "walls got ears in there, you know."

"It's no problem. Do you remember my partner and I coming to speak to you here?"

"No, but I was drinkin' a lot in them days. I been sober now two years."

"Congratulations."

"Thanks. So what do you need?"

"It's about Nina. I've come across some information that makes her life very important for me to scrutinize. I was hoping you could shed some light on it for me."

"I told you guys everythin' last time."

"I thought you didn't remember us coming out?"

"I meant I must've told you guys everythin'. Why wouldn't I have?"

"Sometimes we don't ask the right questions."

He shrugged and folded his arms. "Well ask the right ones then."

"In your initial statement you said that Nina and Mike were having some marital problems. At the time we didn't really follow up on that."

"Um, yeah. From what I remember there was some serious tension there."

"Do you know what it was regarding?"

He looked at him but didn't answer. Stanton remembered that he had dodged this question in the earlier investigation as well.

"Whatever it is," Stanton said, "I've heard worse."

"There just some things that stay in the family, you know? That ain't nobody else's business."

Stanton stepped just a little closer to him. "Dennis, you didn't talk to us much the first time either. And the man that killed them has gone on to kill several others. The information you could've provided might've helped stop that."

"What're you, tryin' to give me a guilt trip? That don't work on me."

166

"I'm not doing anything but informing you of a fact. Dennis, your sister was raped, sodomized, and then murdered. Her children were murdered. How can you not want to do everything in your power to help me catch who did it?"

He pulled out a package of cigarettes from his pocket and lit one, keeping one hand in his pant pocket after replacing the lighter. Stanton let him smoke in silence a long while.

"We all got our troubles, you know? Nina wasn't no different."

"What is it you know exactly, Dennis?"

He blew smoke out of his nose. "She…ah…she was in adult movies."

Stanton's heart dropped. "She was in porn? We didn't see any additional income on her tax statements."

"No, this was all under the table. Her and Mike, they had a website for a while. Just them havin' sex. And then she wanted to try the hard stuff. So she got in with that crowd. They paid her in cash and so she never had to claim any of it."

"Why didn't you tell me this before?" Stanton said, getting within inches of his face.

"Hey, calm the fuck down. Would you wanna go tellin' the world your sister was a whore?"

Stanton shook his head, anger rising inside him. "Do you know how many lives you could've saved if we would've known that?"

"Hey, Officer, I told you everything I know. Now I'm goin' back to work. And what I tell others about family business ain't nobody's right but mine."

He threw the cigarette on the ground, stomped it out, and turned to walk away. Stanton shouted, "What was her porn name?"

Dennis didn't respond as he went back inside and the door shut behind him.

CHAPTER 35

Stanton sat on his balcony, all the girls' files stacked neatly on the sidetable in front of him. There was a pattern now. Nothing was random. The hand of God hadn't just swooped down and chosen for these women to die. This was a deliberate, methodical plan that had been carried out by a man for whom violence and sex had come to mean the same thing.

Nina Blum had been picked because of her work in porn movies. But Stanton had spent an hour on the phone with Vice. Two detectives had researched the entire day and had called back to let him know there wasn't a single person in the adult film industry that had anything to do with every girl. One director had shot two of the girls but not the others, a gaffer had worked with four but not the others…he even had them check caterers and security guards.

Adult film actors and actresses were required to do routine blood testing for sexually transmitted diseases. Some of the girls went to a place called Cutting Edge in Sherman Oaks, but some of them didn't. Nothing fit for all of them.

Stanton stood up and stretched. He had ordered all the girls' financial records. He'd needed to call in a favor with the FBI to get them as quickly as possible but they were more than happy to help. They had been completely shut out of the investigation by the San Diego PD. Several months ago, the FBI had come in and taken credit for one of the largest drug busts in the history of the city and the unofficial policy in the precinct had become non-cooperation.

Stanton went inside and watched television. Then he went

out to his balcony again and decided to go for a walk. He knew sleep was impossible but he was trying his best to not check his email every five minutes.

When the email came, it was four in the morning California time, and seven in the morning in Quantico where the records had been generated. His cell phone buzzed and woke him up. He had fallen asleep on the couch. His neck was stiff and the television was still on, turned to morning cartoons. He turned it off and checked his email.

Stanton was particularly interested in Nina Blum's records but doubted there was anything in her financials since she hid her income from the IRS. He had received them before as part of the initial investigation, but had only gotten her W-2s and credit report. He'd asked for something more in depth this time.

He downloaded the files to his home computer and, after a cold shower to wake him up, began going through credit card statements in detail.

Nothing unusual appeared on her statements except for a charge to "Dr. Morgan's." Stanton googled the term and found a podiatrist, two internists, and a sex store by that name. He clicked on the sex store's link.

Dr. Morgan's Adult Playroom focused on sex toys for couples and singles and claimed to have the largest collection of fetish pornography in the county. Stanton went through the rest of Nina Blum's statements and found twenty-nine purchases there in a twelve-month period.

He minimized the windows. Four other girls had credit cards and he pored through them: all of them had charges to Dr. Morgan's. He had been looking in the wrong place: the connection they all shared wasn't in the porn industry; it was at Dr. Morgan's.

A familiar thrill churned his stomach: something between excitement and fear. Dr. Morgan's didn't open until 9:00 a.m. and he decided he needed to go surfing to kill some time and clear his mind.

The ocean was clear and warm and looked like an enormous

glass surface. Stanton dipped his feet in and sat down. The waves lapped around him and foamed and crackled as he stared out over the horizon.

Hold on, I'm coming for you.

CHAPTER 36

With fifteen minutes to nine, Stanton sat in his car outside of Dr. Morgan's. Gunn was in another car and two uniforms were parked around the block so that the employees wouldn't see them. Stanton's cell phone buzzed: it was Emma. He let it go to voicemail.

A few minutes after nine, a man in blue jeans and a wrinkled denim shirt walked up to the entrance and keyed in a code for the alarm before opening the door. As soon as he was inside, Stanton stepped out of the car. Gunn followed him and nodded to the two officers waiting across the street, and they came over as well.

The interior smelled like incense and the walls were all mirrors. The store was massive, about half the size of a grocery store. Stanton could see aisles filled with clothing, sex toys, lingerie, feminine products, make-up...the aisles went on and on.

The employee came around the corner and his eyes went wide.

"We're going to need to talk," Stanton said.

Dr. Morgan's had five employees not counting the owner, Andrew Mick, who was there most of the time. Gunn got information for all five employees and scheduled them all to come down to Northern for interviews. Only one, the owner, had been resistant, insisting that he wanted to contact his lawyer. Gunn had told him that he could come down now, or call his lawyer after being booked into jail and he agreed to come down.

The first interview was with a young woman with a neck

tattoo. She sat across from Gunn and Stanton in the interrogation room and chewed gum so loudly that spit flew over the table.

Stanton laid out the photographs of all the girls, pushing the one of Nina Blum closest to her.

"Do you recognize these women?"

"Um…some of 'em, yeah."

"Which ones?"

She pointed to Nina Blum, Ashley Low, and Natalie Heath. "These ones."

"How do you know them?"

"They'd come into the store all the time and we'd talk."

"Do you know that Ms. Low is missing and that the other two have been found dead?"

"Yeah," she said, folding her arms, "I heard."

Gunn said, "That's it? You hear your friends are dead and you just say you heard?"

"What d'you want me to say? And they weren't my friends."

"I want you to show some damned compassion."

She scoffed. "You guys aren't Vice. I can tell 'cause you haven't asked me for a blow job. So I'm guessing you don't know anything about the porn game."

Stanton intervened before Gunn could speak again, "I just want to find who hurt these girls. If you know anything that can help me, I would appreciate hearing it now."

"You, I like." She looked to Gunn. "Him I don't."

Stanton glanced to Gunn, hoping he would take the cue. Gunn shrugged and said, "What the fuck do I care what some whore thinks," and stood up and left the room. Stanton waited until the door had shut before speaking.

"I'm sorry. You didn't deserve that. Please tell me what you know."

"I know enough not to be all broken up about them girls. Girls in this game go missing all the time."

"Are you in the industry as well?"

"Yeah, if you can call it that. I mostly do amateur stuff. Just guys that wanna fuck legally so they stick a camera in my face."

"I think these girls were hurt by someone that works at your store or comes to your store often. Do you know anyone like that?"

"The only people that fuck with me at my store are those asshole Vice cops."

"What do they do?"

"They come and threaten all sorts of bullshit like they're gonna close the store down and that I'm gonna be arrested for selling stuff to minors. Then they say if I blow 'em they'll let it slide. Some of the new girls fall for it but I just tell 'em to shove it up their ass."

Stanton took out one of his cards and slid it across the table. "If that ever happens again, I want you to get me their names and call me the second you get a chance. I promise you it won't happen again."

"What are you gonna do?"

"They're not scared of their bosses, cops look out for their own. What they are scared of is exposure. I'll call a friend I have at the *Union-Trib*. They love police corruption stories. Just threatening to do that will be enough for them to never come back to your store."

She grinned. "That's cool."

"Now please tell me: can you think of anyone that could've done something like this?" She glanced up to the camera on the wall. "It's not on," Stanton said.

"Andy, the owner. He's a crazy fucker. He's got a temper and he carries weapons with him. Like guns and knives. He threatened me with a knife once."

"Why didn't you quit?"

"He gave me a raise and apologized. He was just drunk anyway. But that's the only time he's ever gotten crazy with me. One of the other guys told me, though, that Andy had served time once for beatin' a guy to death."

Stanton took a few notes. "Did Andy ever mention anything about any of these girls?"

She glanced over the names. "No, I never heard that."

"Nina had come into the store almost three times a month. What would she buy that she needed to come in there so much?"

"Everything. But mostly clothes and make-up."

"What about the other girls?"

"Same thing. People buy lots of stuff at the store."

"Did the three girls you mentioned ever talk to you about someone that had been following them or someone they were worried about?"

"Like a stalker? No, I don't think so. Nina told me once her husband and her got separated and he followed her around for a long time but that was it. I think they got back together, though."

"Did she say why they separated?"

"He didn't know she was in porn. He found out 'cause some dude at his work told him he'd seen his wife in a porno. He thought he was just making it up. I mean they was swingers anyway so I didn't see the big deal, but Nina said he was pretty pissed when he found out."

"Were any specific customers around when any of these girls were?"

"No, not that I can think of."

"Is there any way for you to get me a list of your regulars? People that are there several times a month?"

"I guess. We got a program that tracks what people buy. You could get that from Andy."

Stanton stood up and opened the door for her. "You're free to leave. Thank you for coming down. I may have some follow-up questions so I'll call you if I do."

She walked toward the door and turned to face him. "You're kinda cute for a cop. If you ever feel like gettin' a little crazy, you should gimmie a call."

Gunn was standing in the hallway. He'd been watching through the one-way glass. "You gonna tap that, Johnny?"

"I wouldn't know what to do with a girl like that."

"She would teach you some things, Jon. That's why I like

them crazy girls. This chick I'm bangin' now, she likes to put warm water in her mouth before blowin' me. You wouldn't believe what a difference that makes."

"Is Andrew here yet?" he said, changing the subject.

"Yeah, he's in room four. Let's go."

CHAPTER 37

Stanton waited outside the interrogation room and watched Andrew Mick. He was an older man. So old that the tattoos that covered his arms and hands were deformed on his sagging skin. His hair was white and he was bald up top. Stanton thought he would look like a grandfather if not for the tattoos and the numerous piercings in his face and ears.

Stanton walked in with Gunn behind him. He sat down while Gunn chose to stand. Stanton wondered if he did it consciously: many studies showed that those that put themselves in physically higher positions were more likely to be seen as intimidating by those in lower positions. For CIA position interviews, the interviewer's chair was always set several inches higher than the interviewee's.

"Sorry to call you down last minute, Andrew," Stanton said. "We wouldn't do it if we didn't think it was absolutely necessary."

"What is this all about?"

Stanton set out the seven photographs. "All these women were abducted and several of them have been found murdered. I've gone through their credit card statements and all seven of them had at least one charge per month at your store."

"Yeah, well, it's a popular store." Andrew glanced over the photos. "Some of these girls are in porno."

"All of them, actually."

"Makes sense."

"Why does that make sense?"

"Deductions."

"What deductions?"

"Tax deductions," Andrew said. "Anything they buy from me is seen as a work expense and is tax deductible if they're in the sex industry. I don't just sell sex toys. We sell clothes, make-up, gym equipment, everything to keep bodies looking good. So a lotta people come to us for everything and then deduct it from their taxes."

Gunn said, "They're claimin' dildos as tax deductions?"

"Hey, man, you save money where you can. With property taxes, sales tax, state and federal, gas, we all paying half our income in taxes. You gotta cut where you can."

"Where were you on June twenty-first of this year?" Stanton said. "Around seven in the evening."

"Where I always am: at the store. I'm there nine to nine Monday through Saturday. You can check with all my employees if you need to."

"What type of car do you drive?"

"A Mercedes C-Class. Why?"

"You don't have a van?"

"You kidding me? What is this, nineteen eighty-one? No I don't have a van. Those things are hideous."

Stanton ran through another half-hour of questions. Throughout the time, Andrew was calm and relaxed. Even when Gunn tried to rattle him with a straight accusation and lied about finding hair fibers in his car, Andrew simply denied it without getting upset.

Finally, Stanton stood up and said, "Don't go anywhere just yet."

He stepped outside and Gunn followed. They stood in the hall and watched Andrew through the glass. He was checking his phone.

"He's too calm," Stanton said. "If he didn't have anything to do with it, he should be more outraged that we're accusing him."

"You think he's our man?"

"I think his employees are going to say he was there on every date the girls went missing." Stanton paced the floor. "I want to bring in Dillon and see if he can ID Andrew."

"I'm on it."

Stanton brought a soda in to Andrew and told him it would be a while since they were following up on some of the things he said. He sat across from him and sipped an orange juice.

"How did you get into this industry?" Stanton asked.

"I love sex. They say you gotta open a business you love."

"Do you enjoy it as much as you thought you would?"

He shrugged. "Not really. But what're you gonna do? That's life I guess."

"Why a sex shop instead of getting into porn if you love sex?"

"I did for a while. Three films in the eighties. Wasn't my scene, though. That's right when AIDS was making the rounds and most people in the industry didn't want to wear condoms."

"Why not?"

"The directors and studio execs didn't want it. See a porno is a fantasy. It's not real. The girls are dressed and made up in a way they normally aren't. The moans and groans are fake; the dialogue is fake. And so they didn't want to ruin the fantasy with condoms. Videos with condoms sell less than the ones that don't have 'em. I've seen that in my store too. People have to wear condoms in real life; they don't want to see it in their fantasies too."

Stanton sipped some more juice. "You're much more insightful about your industry than I thought you would be."

"I'm in it for the right reasons." He leaned forward. "Let me ask you something; you guys really think I'm the guy that killed these girls?"

"I don't know yet."

He nodded. "An honest answer. You're not the first cop I've dealt with. I appreciate that."

"I've heard you've had some problems with Vice."

"They're always shaking me down for money. Sometimes they get sex outta my girls but that hasn't been too much of a problem since I got cameras installed everywhere. I held off on that for a long time 'cause I figured my customers wouldn't like being on video, but times change."

"Have you ever thought of filing complaints?"

"Against Vice? It'd just be my word against theirs. Who's gonna believe me over them?"

Commotion outside made them both look toward the one-way glass, but all they saw were their reflections looking back at them.

"Excuse me," Stanton said. He went outside to see Gunn standing behind Dillon.

"That ain't him," Dillon said.

"How do you know?" Gunn said.

"The dude didn't have tats on his neck."

"You're sure?" Gunn said.

"Yeah. And the fucker was bigger than this guy. He was really big. Like a football player or something."

Stanton looked to Gunn and then back to Dillon.

"All right, you can go," Gunn said.

"Hey, man, you dragged me here. I need a ride home."

"I'll call you a cab."

Stanton watched Andrew, who was on his phone again. He went into the room and opened the door all the way.

"You're free to go, Andrew."

CHAPTER 38

Stanton sat in a coffee shop in La Jolla near the beach. From the table he was sitting at he could see the ocean, and he sipped an Italian soda with his iPad open in front of him. He stared at the screen a while before searching for accountants in Southern California. He called the first firm in the search results.

"McCain, Debner and McCullagh, this is Cindy. How may I help you?"

"I'd like to speak to one of your accountants please."

"And what is this regarding?"

"A police investigation."

"Um...just one second."

A click and a male voice.

"This is Richard."

"Yes, Richard, my name is Jon Stanton. I'm a consultant for the San Diego Police Department. I'm helping them with a case right now and just have a quick question for you."

"Shoot."

"If someone were working in the sex industry, like pornography, would anything they buy at a sex shop in furtherance of their profession be tax deductible? Like lingerie and make-up and things?"

"Hm, you know I've never had anyone ask me that. I'd have to look it up, but off the top of my head, I wouldn't think so. Maybe the studio could claim it was tax deductible."

"I see. Well, thank you for your time."

Stanton hung up and looked at his phone a moment before calling the second number on the search results. The answer was nearly identical. He called several more accountants: none of them knew for certain whether such items would be tax deductible. It wasn't common knowledge. He wondered if the porn industry let their stars know or whether they passed the knowledge among themselves.

Stanton's phone buzzed. It was Gunn.

"What'd you find out?" Stanton asked.

"Andrew's a sick fuck but he checks out. All the other employees said he's there every day from nine to nine, just like you said they would. So either they're lying or it's not him. Childs and I hit up everyone that worked there. None of 'em fit. Most of 'em are women and the one guy that works there had alibis that checked out for most of the dates we're lookin' for."

Stanton leaned back in the chair. "I was so sure that store was the connection between them. I'm not convinced about Andrew, though."

"You ask me, that's too much of a coincidence that all our vics shopped at the same store. There's gotta be somethin' there."

"I'm sure there is. We're just not looking in the right place."

"Well the employees don't clean the place. Andrew hires a cleaning company to come in twice a week. I'm gonna run through the folks comin' in from there. And I'll keep digging on Andrew. If he told his employees to lie, one of 'em's gonna break."

"Keep me posted."

"Sure."

Stanton hung up and placed the phone down on the tabletop. He watched several of the patrons at the coffee shop. Most of them were college students and it took him back to his own college days of cramming for exams and attending study groups.

Though he had received his graduate degree in psychology, another area of emphasis he had specialized in was mathematical modeling. He always loved mathematics and believed that though psychology was not a science—yet—through the use of proper modeling and statistical analysis, it could gain the status of a hard science. It wouldn't happen in his lifetime, but it could happen if psychology produced the equivalent of a Newton or an Einstein.

One model that came up again and again in criminal analysis was the rooted, or hierarchical, tree model. It was used frequently in computer science and consisted of one node, say a number, that branched out like a tree to different numbers. The nodes were all ranked in accordance with their distance from the root node. The closer to the root, the higher the ranking. Each node closer to the root was termed the parent node of one farther away. And the node closest to the root was the highest ranked.

Stanton had applied this model to serial murder. He believed it was the secret to his high rate of closed cases, and why he was routinely mistaken for having some sort of extrasensory perception. But he simply modeled the murders using this root system. The killer was the root, and each victim's importance was ranked depending on its distance in time from the root. The first victim was then the most important, as they were always closest to the root. Often the killer coveted this victim and even knew them on a personal level.

The node closest to the killer here was Nina Blum. Though Stanton had no doubt that the man he was after had participated with Oster in all the murders, Nina Blum was his first solo. Her murder was the purest expression of his pathology. Though he was evolving and had already done so with Natalie Heath, Nina Blum was an expression of his unconscious, like an abstract painting that leads back to layers and layers of meaning in the artist's psyche.

Stanton pulled up the Nina Blum file again. He'd scanned it and sent it to his iPad: something he preferred not to do since he felt paper files were superior, but hauling around thick murder books to coffee shops was something he didn't dare try.

He stared at the crime-scene photos. The inhumanity of her death exposed sympathy in him every time he looked at her photos. She had been alive well after her family had been killed. He wondered if at that point she had even cared to fight for her life.

He began going through her financials again. That was where the answer was. It was through Andrew's sex shop, but he didn't know where. She had filed taxes jointly with her husband and no additional income had been claimed. Stanton scanned through their deductions until he reached the bottom of the page. His plan was to call her accountant and ask about the sex shop deductions.

He saw the signature of the accountant at the bottom and then glanced up to the printed name. It said, JAMES F. HILDER, CPA. Hilder and Gilchrest.

Stanton googled him and saw the link for his bio page on the accounting firm's website. Hilder and Gilchrest sounded familiar and he wasn't sure why.

He clicked on Hilder's profile and read through it quickly before going to the other accountants'. His heart dropped as he remembered why he had heard that firm name before: the fourth accountant down from the top was Kyle S. Bonnie.

Stanton tried to calm himself as he accessed the tax returns of every other girl. The signing accountants were either James Hilder or Nassen Gilchrest.

He closed his iPad and dashed out of the coffee shop.

CHAPTER 39

Alone in his office, Kyle Bonnie sat at his desk with a legal pad on his lap. His feet were up and he'd taken his shoes off. For a long time, he admired his custom-made socks with gold trim. They had cost more than many people's suits.

He was scribbling on the pad and would stop every so often to admire his drawings. He thought one in particular was good enough to keep: it was of a girl with her head torn from her body, the blood spilling down over her headless torso. He ripped it out and went to fold it up but instead just threw it in the trash. He then began drawing various bones and skulls with ragged flesh coming off them. He drew maybe fifty of them on the page and the chaos of the ink on the yellow paper made him smile.

"Mr. Bonnie?"

He looked up, startled to see his secretary, Heather, standing there. Bonnie turned the legal pad upside down and placed it on his desk.

"What is it?"

"Um, your ten o'clock is here. Jenna something."

"I remember. Just call me next time."

"Your phone didn't pick up."

Bonnie looked to his phone and saw that it was disabled; he didn't remember doing that. He enabled it and put his shoes back on. "Send her in."

A few moments later a brunette in a violet dress walked in. She wore black high heels with leather straps wrapped around her ankles. Her nails were painted purple with white tips.

"How are you, Jenna?" Bonnie said, standing and shaking her

hand.

"Good. How have you been?"

"Fine. Fine as can be I guess."

"Kyle, you didn't have to meet me. I know everything that's going on with Jill...and I don't know what I'm trying to say. Just, I understand if you need time off from the biz."

"No, it's fine. You guys are my best clients. Besides, throwing myself into work helps me forget what's going on everywhere else." He exhaled. "So, you had some questions about forming your own company."

"Yeah, basically what I want is a company owned by me, completely separate from the studio. And then I'll have a website where my fans can put in requests for me to do things on the webcam, like girl-girl or anal or whatever."

"How long do you have left on your contract with the studio?"

"Two years. My attorney's trying to work wit—"

Bonnie's phone rang. "Excuse me." It was his secretary. "I'm in a damned meeting," he said. When he saw Jenna's face, he softened. "I have a very important client, Heather. So please hold the rest of my calls until I'm finished."

"Okay, I just thought—"

"No, you didn't think. Now please hold all my calls."

"Yes, sir. It was just that cop, but I'll talk to you after your meeting."

"What cop?"

"That one that came in here to speak to you about Jill."

"Jon Stanton."

"Yeah, him."

"Well what did he want?"

"He asked if you were in and I told him you were."

"That's it? He didn't want to speak to me?"

"No, I think he just wanted to know if you were here. I think he's coming down."

"Did he say anything else?"

"Um, oh, he asked about your tattoo...Mr. Bonnie? You still

there?"

"I'm still here. What about my tattoo?"

"He asked if you had any on your arms and I told him you had that bull tattoo from when you were in the Army."

"You told him that, huh? Well you're just a wiseass bitch, aren't you?"

Jenna stood, "I should go."

"No, wait, Jenna," Bonnie slammed the phone down. "Look, I'll come over to your house later and we can talk."

"Um, I'll call you."

Bonnie sat quietly at his desk as he watched her walk out. His sleeves were buttoned and he unbuttoned them and stared at the large Minotaur on his forearm, the corpses of women at his hooved feet.

Calmly, he took the .40 caliber Ruger out of his top drawer, put on his suit coat, which had been on a coatrack behind him, and walked out of his office into the lobby. Heather looked up at him just as he fired. The round went through her right eye and a spray of blood rained over her desk.

The shot was loud enough that the people in the surrounding offices stuck their heads out to see what was going on. Bonnie fired at two of them and people began to scream and run.

He followed them out. James Hilder came out of his office, a look of panic and confusion on his face.

"Hey, Jim," Bonnie shouted, raising the weapon, "I quit."

He fired twice, watching the body hit the floor, and ran out of the building.

CHAPTER 40

Stanton rushed up the street and came to a screeching stop in front of the office building that housed Hilder and Gilchrest. Several police cruisers and the SWAT team were already there. He saw Childs and Gunn on the sidewalk as SWAT took the operation over. The red and blues of several ambulances flickered in the morning light.

He ran over to them and a uniform wouldn't let him pass until Childs came over and waved him through. Gunn laughed at him.

"What happened?" Stanton said.

"Your boy," Childs responded, looking up to the building. "Decided to shoot the place up. Killed two people."

"Where is he?"

"He's gone, man. I got a BOLO out on him right now, and we got uniforms at his house and his girlfriend's house."

"Have someone call Homeland Security and put an alert on his passport. He's not sticking around."

"Any idea where he's goin'?"

"No. But I bet I know someone that might."

Stanton waited an hour and half in the lobby of the George Bailey Maximum Security Correctional Complex for the guards to bring out Philip Oster. Every second was agonizing. He pictured Kyle Bonnie on a cruise ship heading to Mexico, flirting with the women on board whose bodies could disappear into the ocean without a trace.

They wouldn't let Stanton see Oster and he'd had to put a

call in to Childs, who called the assistant chief of police. Even then, he had to wait until Oster was properly prepped. Apparently he was in solitary confinement for stabbing another inmate in the throat with a fork.

Oster came out and Stanton was amazed the difference even a short time in solitary could make. He was thin and appeared greasy and dirty. He sat down across from him but didn't speak or smile. He didn't show any reaction at all other than squinting at the overhead lights.

"You doing okay?" Stanton said.

"No, Detective Stanton. I am certainly not doing fucking okay. You know they only feed you once a day in solitary and whatever food they got they mix shit into it? I mean shit. Feces. Or urine. The food's prepared by inmates in the kitchen and they know you can't do nothin' to them so they fuck with you."

"I'm sorry, Philip. I really am."

"You know what's fucked up? I actually believe you. That you feel sorry for me. Why would you do that?"

"I'd be happy to explain it to you another time. But I have a favor to ask right now."

"You wanna know where Kyle's goin', don't you?"

Stanton was silent. "How did you...never mind. It doesn't matter. Can you tell me where he is?"

"No, I don't know where he is."

"Do you know where he's going?"

"That I might know. If the price is right."

"What do you want?"

"I've already told you and that cunt at the DA's Office: I want minimum security."

"You're a serial murderer who just attacked another inmate. If all you want is a promise, the DA's Office can give you that, but it won't happen. You know it won't happen."

He sighed. "Then I'm afraid Kyle's in the wind, Detective."

"I'm not a detective, Philip. I've told you that."

"No, you are. Just like I'm a criminal, man. Seems like you're born into what you do."

"What else can I offer you?"

"Don't want nothin' else."

"There has to be something. Eventually he's going to get away and you won't have any leverage. You should use it now while you have it."

He thought a moment. "Good point. All right, I'll take you to where he is. But I'll take you personally. You can cuff and chain me, whatever. But I want to take you personally."

"Why?"

"I'm sick a solitary. I want out, even for a day." He leaned forward. "I'll take you right to him, Detective. And I'm willin' to bet he's got another girl up there with him who probably don't have too long." He stood up and nodded to the guard, who came and took him by the elbow. "And I want minimum security. A deal in writing to my attorney. In exchange, you get your man and save the life of the girl he's got right now. Think about it, Detective. I think you know where to find me."

CHAPTER 41

Stanton sat in the lobby outside Kathleen Ackerman's office. Kathleen was in a meeting with her boss, discussing everything Stanton had explained over the phone. She thought it would be better if she pitched it to him first.

His cell phone rang. It was Emma.

"Hey," Stanton said. "How's Boston?"

"Cold and it's the middle of summer. Maybe it's just because I'm used to the heat of LA."

"Have you seen any of the sights?"

"I graduated from MIT, Jon. I've seen the sights."

"Oh, that's right. I forgot about that."

"You okay?"

"Just a little distracted. How's the symposium going?"

"Bunch of old men talking about chemistry. As big a party as you can expect."

He hesitated. "I miss you."

"I miss you too. Why don't you fly out here today and join me? We can go hit all the museums."

"I can't right now. I'm...I just can't right now, Emma."

"I understand," she said softly.

He exhaled. "I'm sorry. I'm so sorry I broke my promise to you. I should've never gotten involved with this case. And you're right. There'll just be others after this one. I can't chase after them all."

"So no more cases after this?"

"I think I need to get out of the realm altogether. As a PI, I have one foot in and one foot out. That'll never work. I have to have a clean break from this."

"Do you thin—"

"Jon," Kathleen said, poking her head out of her office, "can you join us?"

"I have to go, Em. I'll call you tonight."

"Okay...I love you."

"I love you too."

Two men were in Kathleen's office: her direct supervisor, Vince Goldburg, and his boss, Senior Assistant District Attorney Kenneth Nelson. Stanton chose to stand rather than sit in between them.

"I've told them what we've been talking about," Kathleen said.

"We have some concerns," Nelson said. "We contacted Mr. Oster's attorney and there were additional stipulations."

"Like what?"

"Mr. Oster would like you to accompany the party that he leads to Kyle Bonnie."

"Fine. If it'll get us Bonnie."

"He would also like a meal at McDonald's, which I think is doable. We could just eat in the transport van. But he also wants to be able to write a book about his experiences."

"What's wrong with that?" Stanton asked.

"Well, nothing initially. But there's a Supreme Court case prohibiting criminals from making money off their stories in the media, if the victims or the victims' families object. Well, the victims' families are going to object."

"And he wants you to convince the families to let him keep the money?" Stanton asked.

"Correct. You can see our dilemma."

Kathleen said, "I know two of the families would never agree. No matter what."

"Even if you explained to them that the man we're looking for is at least partly responsible for the death of their loved one?"

"I called one of them. They said they would never sign a release that lets Oster become a millionaire for talking about the death of their daughter. And I don't blame them."

Stanton began to pace. "There's another Supreme Court case that says you don't have to uphold any bargain, if I remember right."

"That's correct," Nelson said. "But you can imagine what that'll do to our reputation when Henry Grimes goes on the news and describes in detail how we lied to him and his client. I don't think many defense attorneys would be willing to trust us again."

Stanton walked to the window. "Oster has a stepfather. The stepfather can write it." He turned to them. "The law prohibits the convict from writing it, not their relatives. The stepfather can write it and cite inside sources. They're just going to get a ghost writer anyway. He can have several interviews with Oster in the book. It'll sell nearly as much."

The men looked at each other.

Kathleen said, "I'll take it to Grimes and see what he says. Stay by your phone. If he accepts, I want to go out tomorrow."

Nelson gave her a disapproving look. "I'd like more time to prepare security adequately."

"He might already have another girl. Or be on his way out of the country. I don't think we have any time to wait. Jon, do you agree?"

"She's right. He could already be gone. I just need two other officers. We'll keep him in double-locked cuffs and ankle braces. He won't be going anywhere. And you guys are okay with his requirement for minimum security?"

"There's a screw up there," Nelson said, "and it's the jail's deal. Not ours. I have no problem with that, but if he so much as doesn't clean his cell, he'll be going back to max."

"Minimum security isn't set up for guys like him. He could escape."

Nelson thought a moment and then stood up. "We'll arrange a press release with your names on it. This blows up, it's your baby."

The two men walked out and Stanton sat down. Kathleen rose, shut the door, and collapsed into her chair with a sigh.

"The joys of government work," she said.

"You know if something goes wrong, they could fire you for this. Why are you putting your job on the line?"

"I started as a sex crimes prosecutor. I have a soft spot for the girls in the sex industries."

"And if it does work, you'll be interviewed by every major news station in the country."

She smiled. "Be honest with me, Jon. Why did you quit? Few more years and you could've moved out of field work and into administration anyway."

"It's more about covering your butt now than catching perps. It's not why I went into it." He rose. "Call me and let me know as soon as you talk to Grimes."

CHAPTER 42

For the first time in several years, Philip Oster saw the sunrise without being caged behind walls. He stood on the outside of the prison, at the front entrance, with a federal marshal on either side of him. His handcuffs were thicker than any he'd ever seen and the chain locked to them reached down to the cuffs on his ankles.

Jon Stanton and Stephen Gunn came to a stop in front of the prison in a transport van loaned to them from San Diego County. Stanton got out and slid open the side door.

"Federal marshals," Oster said. "I'm impressed you got 'em on such short notice."

Stanton didn't respond as he helped Oster into the van and the marshals locked him into his seat. Gunn turned around in the passenger seat to look at Oster.

"See this?" Gunn said, taking out his firearm. "I'm gonna put this on my lap. You fuck around, I'm puttin' a bullet through your mouth. And every cop and prosecutor in this county will thank me for it. Capiche?"

"Not as pleasant as you, is he, Jon?"

Stanton got into the driver's seat and started the van.

The directions Oster gave them only took them about a quarter of the way to their destination. He said he didn't want them just dumping him off and going up without him.

They began heading north on I-15 and it was still early enough in the morning, around 6:00 a.m., that traffic was light.

"I heard about you, Detective Gunn," Oster said. "People inside know you really well. You better not ever do time for nothin' 'cause I don't think you got a lotta friends in there."

"Shut up, you piece a shit."

"No, no, I'm not sayin' me. I'm as friendly as can be, Detective. I'm sayin' you got some bad dudes in there that feel they don't deserve to be in there except that you planted evidence or raided their houses without warrants."

Stanton glanced to Gunn and then back out onto the road.

Gunn said, "You find out about this from pillow talk, Philip? I'm curious, you a bottom or a top? You look like a bottom to me."

Oster said calmly, "You ever been raped by another man, Detective Gunn? If you had, I don't think it'd be somethin' you'd be laughin' about. Maybe I can show you sometime?"

One of the marshals yanked on Oster's cuffs and told him to keep it down. Stanton turned on a radio station to try to dissuade conversation.

The drive was long and tedious and they had to stop for gas once. Oster insisted he had to use the bathroom and both marshals went with him while Gunn stood outside the restroom door with his hand on his weapon like he was in a Wild West film.

After three and a half hours of driving, they had left civilization and were now near Joshua Tree National Park. Desert stretched out before them and rolled into hills and open blue sky. Oster directed them up a winding road, and past several hills with cabins interspersed on top of them. The road got more difficult as it inclined steeply and massive rock formations began to encircle them.

"It's up here on the right," Oster said.

Stanton pulled up and stopped in front of a large cabin with only a few windows.

"Nice," Gunn said. "How'd he afford a place like this?"

"Real estate investments in the eighties. Before everything went to shit," Oster said.

"We'll call in the location," Stanton said.

"What're you kiddin' me?" Gunn turned to him. "We're three hours from our home turf. You know how long it's gonna take SWAT to get it together and get up here."

"Childs is waiting for our call. And we need the local Sheriff's Office involved too."

"No fucking way. I'm not lettin' a bunch of commandos from SWAT get the credit for this takedown. This is us, all the way."

"No. We're waiting. And I'm not even a cop anymore. I don't have a gun."

Gunn reached down to his ankle and pulled out his backup piece. He handed it to Stanton. "There, now you're armed."

Gunn hopped out of the van before Stanton could say anything. He knew he was going into that cabin with or without him.

"See," Oster said, "he does things without thinkin'. That's what gets him into trouble."

"What's in there, Philip?"

"Kyle. Probably asleep. That's assuming he hasn't already gone to Mexico. And maybe a little trophy girl to keep him busy."

"Anybody else?"

"Nope. Kyle didn't make friends easy."

Stanton watched as Gunn approached the house. He said to the marshals, "If he moves, shoot him," before getting out and following Gunn.

CHAPTER 43

The cabin appeared out of place. Stanton couldn't see another one anywhere near here and the property seemed worthless: just an expanse of desert out in the middle of nowhere. The sun beat down on him and he felt beads of sweat after being out only a few minutes.

"I could be surfing right now," Stanton said. "Why do I do this to myself, Stephen?"

"Because you love the adrenaline. Same as me."

Approaching the entrance to the cabin, Gunn motioned for Stanton to go around back. He did and found an unlocked backdoor. Only the screen was locked and he quickly snapped the fragile lock and went inside. A warrant had been issued for Kyle Bonnie and he had authority to enter, but Childs had the warrant back in San Diego. He wouldn't be able to show it to Bonnie if he asked for it, which might cause some problems later in court if he hired a knowledgeable attorney. Then again, Stanton wasn't a police officer and anything he found would be admissible, though they might charge him with breaking and entering into a private dwelling.

The cabin was large and decorated in a Western motif. Bearskin rugs and trophy heads and old rifles were up on the walls. The bare floors creaked with every step. It smelled like dust, as if no one had been through here in a long time.

Stanton, gun first, made his way through the kitchen. He kept his breathing shallow and his back to a wall whenever he could. By the time he got to the living room, sweat was pouring out of him and stinging his eyes. He had forgotten what this felt like.

He unlocked the front door, and let Gunn inside.

Gunn motioned upstairs and Stanton shook his head, indicating it hadn't been cleared. Gunn began to take the stairs leading up while Stanton circled around to the kitchen and then to the two bedrooms on this floor.

The cabin appeared like something out of a magazine and at first glance Stanton was impressed with its décor. Then he noticed that there wasn't a single personal item in the home. Everything seemed as if it was ordered out of a catalogue. No photos, no clothing, not even food in the kitchen.

He looked through the cabinets and the drawers, trying to remain as quiet as possible. A few forks and spoons and knives with a couple of dusty plates, but nothing else. He heard steps coming down from upstairs and he went back out front.

"No one's home," Gunn said. "I think Philip's bullshitting us."

"I don't think so."

"Why?"

"This house is too perfect. It's inaccessible and you'd see someone coming from miles away."

"Then where's Bonnie?"

"Probably fled the state. But he's spent time here. That means there's something we're missing. A room. Somewhere for him to keep his clothes and his computer, things like that."

"There're two bedrooms and a bathroom upstairs. That's it."

Stanton turned to the kitchen. Gunn followed him as he went in. Stanton moved the rug that was beneath the kitchen table. Nothing but more floor. He went to the first bedroom and checked under the bed. It was empty space.

Stanton stood still and listened to the cabin. Behind the walls, he could hear scratching and creaking, likely from mice, as if a lot of space was back there for things to move around in. He walked to the closet: it was full of junk. A dresser inside took up most of the space.

"Help me move this."

They moved the dresser out and found a three-foot metal

THE PORN STAR MURDERS

grate on the wall. Stanton bent down and looked into it but could only see darkness.

"See anything?" Gunn asked.

"No. I think this comes off."

He pulled at the top of the grate and it groaned as it came away from the wall.

"Wish we had a flashlight," Stanton said.

"I think I saw those marshals carryin' some on their belts. I'll grab one."

Stanton sat back and brought his knees to his chest. He looked into what was just a large hole. It was at least three feet high and about as wide. Fear tingled in his belly as he imagined what he could find on the other side. He decided they weren't going in on their own; they would wait for backup like they should have done in the first place.

Air wafted out of the hole. It had a rotten-egg smell but wasn't overpowering. Stanton figured they would find trophies from Bonnie's kills. Jewelry and underwear were usually the items taken from victims, but some killers preferred organic material and took nails or teeth or fingers with them.

A noise came from the hole. Stanton froze, his heart pounding in his chest. He was suddenly glad Gunn had given him a firearm. He remained motionless a while until he heard it again.

Stanton crawled over to the hole and listened. Deep inside the home somewhere, he could hear a voice.

It was too faint to tell whether it was male or female, but it was whining, as if in pain. He listened a long time and the noise didn't stop. He could faintly make out what it was saying: help.

He glanced out the window to see if Gunn was near, but he was leaning against the van, talking to the marshals.

Taking a deep breath, he tucked the firearm into his waistband, and crawled into the darkness of the hole.

CHAPTER 44

As Stanton crawled farther in, he noticed two things: the smell grew stronger and more putrid, and the voice grew louder. He was going in the right direction. The hole appeared to have been built as an addition after the house was complete. It wasn't smooth but was smaller and larger in different areas.

Stanton crawled about fifteen feet before coming to a turn. The faint light behind him didn't help much and after the turn there was nothing.

"Jon?"

"Stephen, throw me the flashlight."

Stanton heard the metal as the flashlight rolled toward him. He backed up enough to retrieve it and turned it on.

The hole tilted down, underground. It had been dug underneath the home and then encased in concrete. But the job had been done too quickly and the concrete was coming off in parts and dirt was sprinkling down into the crawlspace.

Stanton glanced back to Gunn, who was now behind him and gave him a look that said, *What the hell are you doing?* Stanton said, "I heard a voice. Did you put the call in for backup?"

"Yeah. SWAT's two and half hours away."

The voice resurfaced from the darkness. It was attempting to say something but it was muffled and Stanton couldn't understand. "We can't wait."

Gunn had stopped crawling. "Hey, Jon. I never told you this, but I'm claustrophobic, man. I can't be crawlin' around in no tunnel."

Stanton ignored him and continued toward the voice.

As he rounded the turn, another turn immediately appeared, this one in the other direction. He followed it down, the stench becoming unbearable. He had smelled it enough in his life to know exactly what it was: decay. Decay and death.

Within twenty seconds, Stanton came to a fork. The tunnel split to the left and to the right and the voice had stopped. He listened quietly, holding his breath, and then shouted, "I can't hear you. Please say something."

But there was only silence now. Stanton leaned to the left and shone the flashlight but couldn't see anything. He did the same to the right with the same result. He turned the flashlight off and smelled the air. Each sense was more acute when the other ones were deprived of stimulation so he closed his eyes and plugged his ears.

The scent of decay seemed to be stronger on the left. He turned the flashlight on and followed it down. He heard the voice again. It was incomprehensible; a string of pleading. Stanton quickened his pace.

The tunnel contracted to within a few inches around him. He had to stop a moment to close his eyes and think of the beach. He thought of the warm waves lapping his wetsuit and the feel of the first wave of the day as it propelled him toward shore. He felt the heat of the sun on his face and the warm sand between his toes as he walked back up the sand and smelled the frying meat from the taco stand in the parking lot.

He began to crawl again, and the tunnel felt like it was constricting him, trying to drain the life out of him. Just at the moment when he was considering turning back, it began to open.

As he continued to crawl, he could see a dim light up ahead. It was a warm glow but didn't appear like a lightbulb. He could hear the voice clearly now: it was a female, and she was crying.

As abruptly as it had closed around him, the tunnel opened up to a wide opening of about four feet. Stanton could see lit candles on a table against a far wall. He checked around the lip of the hole, and then crawled out to his feet.

CHAPTER 45

Daniel Childs sat in the back of the unmarked van and checked his emails on his phone. Everyone wanted constant updates on the Kyle Bonnie apprehension. He had sent out a few emails to his boss, Assistant Chief Ho, and expected him to send them to the appropriate people. But that didn't happen, and he found himself replying to over twenty emails.

"Did we find 'em?" Childs said to the driver.

"Yeah, just got off the phone with Detective Gunn. He gave me directions."

"How far away?"

"About twenty minutes from us. But SWAT's over two hours away back in San Diego."

Childs shook his head. His van had been following the one carrying Oster but had lost it on a turn in Joshua Tree. Gunn hadn't answered his phone in over half an hour.

Childs had requested that SWAT follow them in unmarked vans but that wasn't procedure and they weren't comfortable with it. SWAT was like a nuclear weapon you only brought out when you had to, and the higher-ups hadn't wanted them driving around for several hours fully armed. It had probably been a liability issue, but Childs thought that it might have something to do with PR as well. The image of vans full of heavily armored police going through their neighborhoods might make some people uncomfortable. Even uncomfortable enough to contact the mayor or their legislators, or worse, the media, and then the chief would have to spend hours convincing them that everything was fine and that this was a one-time thing.

"Um, Lieutenant?" the driver said.

"Yeah."

"I think you should talk to Detective Gunn."

He got up to the front of the van and took the phone. "Stephen, what'chyu got?"

"We got a tunnel underneath the house. Jon went in without me."

"What the hell did he go in for? Your orders were to wait for backup."

"I know, I told him that. He said he wasn't a cop no more and could do whatever he wanted."

Childs exhaled. "Get your ass into that house and extract him. Now. I can't have a fuckin' civilian killed during this."

"I tried, Danny. I was just in there. He wouldn't listen."

"Well pull out your weapon and place him under arrest. You are a cop, aren't you?"

"Ten four."

Childs hung up and handed the phone back. "Speed it up. We need to be there yesterday."

Kathleen Ackerman sat in her office, staring out the window. She was biting her thumbnail when Nelson walked in and sat across from her.

"You look nervous."

"I am nervous."

"Nervous that they're going to find Kyle Bonnie or that they're not going to find Kyle Bonnie?"

"Both," she said, placing her arms down on her desk. "Did we do the right thing?"

"Absolutely."

"Jon's not stupid. Once he figures it out, he's going to be pissed. Law suit pissed."

"Law suit for what? Lying to him? We can lie all we want. And he's never going to find out so you have nothing to worry about." He crossed his legs. "I missed you last night."

"I had to catch up on work."

"That seems to be happening more and more."

"I'm just busy, Ken. You don't want me this busy, don't give me so many cases. You know plenty of other DDAs."

"You're good at what you do. I have to give the cases to whoever I think can work them properly." He hesitated. "Are you coming over tonight? Because if not, I'm getting the impression that maybe you're seeing someone else too."

"Can we just focus on one thing at a time? Two of our own are risking their lives right now."

Ken adjusted his tie and stood up. "They're not our own. Especially Jon Stanton." He walked to the door and then turned around. "I expect to see you at my house by ten. Please be there."

After he had left, Kathleen leaned back in her seat. She wished she had never gotten involved with Ken Nelson. She had heard stories about him. That he seduced girls at the office and then left them high and dry when he got bored. But she wasn't a girl, and she had gotten bored before he did. Worried about her job, she debated whether she should just call it off or be so distant that he would lose interest.

She pushed the thoughts out of her mind and stared at the window again. Unconsciously, her thumbnail came back up to her mouth.

CHAPTER 46

Stanton turned off his flashlight and waited until his eyes adjusted to the light before moving. He pressed his back against the wall and held his firearm low. He could hear sobbing now, off to his left, but he couldn't see anything. He brought his shirt up over his nose. The smell was so intense he had to fight the urge to dry heave.

He made his way along the wall toward the sobbing. Something hit his shoe and he stopped. He tried to feel it through his sole. It was smooth and about a foot and a half in length with bulbous ends. Reaching down and touching it with his hand, he knew what it was almost immediately: a human femur bone. Gently, he brushed it aside and continued toward the sobbing.

The wall came to an end and he felt the corner's edge as he turned and followed the new wall. The sobbing was loud. His path was suddenly blocked by something waist-high. He felt along the edge: it was a metal table. He touched its surface and came upon something warm that moved to the touch. Bringing up the flashlight, he flipped it on.

A young woman was bound with duct tape on a metal gurney, nude and covered with urine and fecal matter. Her legs were taped at the ankles and wrists behind her. A rope around her waist was connected to a metal hook on the wall, the walls nothing more than wood nailed up to keep the dirt from collapsing inside. Stanton looked right into her eyes but she didn't respond: she was in shock.

Stanton leaned down and whispered, "I'm with the police. I'm going to get you out. But I need you to stay quiet."

He began pulling the duct tape off. He could see the results of the abuse she had suffered and couldn't imagine the horror she'd been through. He pushed it out of his mind and helped her off the table.

"Please get me outta here, please," she cried.

"I will. We have to go through the tunnel."

"No!" she screamed. "No, please."

"Okay, it's okay. Calm down. We'll go when you're ready."

"No, no, please."

Stanton swung his flashlight around the room. "Is there another way out?"

She shook her head. "I don't know. He would...he would..."

"It's okay," he said, gently putting his arm around her. She flinched and he could feel the tension in her shoulders. "The room goes on in that direction. Wait here and I'll see if—"

"No! Please don't leave me, please," she said, clinging to him now as if she were drowning.

"Okay, it's okay. I won't leave. I won't leave you. We'll wait for—"

"Is that Jon Stanton? Hello, Jon."

Stanton held up the firearm, swinging around blindly in the dark. The flashlight could only illuminate about six feet and past that it was pitch black, broken only by the dim candlelight.

"Okay," Stanton said, "we need to leave now. Come on."

"No, please. I can't go back in there."

"We have to. Just go up ahead of me. I'll be right behind you."

The voice shouted, "I wouldn't do that, Jon. I got enough dynamite here to blow this whole house to hell. You'll be buried here, with me."

Stanton stared at the hole and the tunnel leading out to an awaiting van. He considered the possibility that he was lying, that there was no dynamite.

"He's telling the truth," the girl said, still sobbing.

"How do you know?"

"I saw him bring boxes in and he said they were dynamite. That if I tried to escape he would trap me down here."

Stanton leaned in close. "What's your name?"

"Jess...Jessica."

"Jessica, I need you to listen to me: you need to get into that tunnel and crawl through it. At the other end, in the house, is a detective named Stephen Gunn. Tell him I'm down here with Kyle Bonnie and that Bonnie has dynamite. Tell him to take you and get out of the house as fast as possible."

"I can't...I can't."

"You can be afraid later," he whispered. "Do you understand? You are allowed to be afraid but tell yourself that you will feel it later, after you get out of the tunnel. Can you do that?"

She sobbed quietly, her hand, black with dirt and bleeding, covering her mouth. She nodded and Stanton led her to the hole. Stanton took off his shirt and put it on her. He buttoned it and rolled up the sleeves before helping her into the hole. She wept softly at the entrance, and then began to slowly crawl on her belly. Stanton turned to the darkness. He could hear breathing not far from him.

CHAPTER 47

Gunn sat in the van and surfed the internet on his phone. Periodically, he'd glance up to the house and then back to his phone. Oster was sitting behind him and the two marshals were just outside the van doors, smoking.

"He musta really pissed you off," Oster said.

"What'd you say, you piece a shit?"

"I said he musta really pissed you off for you to leave him in there by himself."

"Shut your fuckin' mouth."

"Can you go one sentence without swearin'?"

"Fuck you."

Oster shrugged. "Suit yourself. Don't talk to me. But I heard you on the phone. It sounded like you were ordered to go in there and get Jon. Seems like your bosses would be pretty pissed if he got hurt in there."

"Yeah, and what would you know about it?"

"I know you. I've spoken with enough people you put away to know what kind of man you are. The kind that's gonna let his partner die in there by himself."

"He ain't my partner."

"No, he's not. He's better than you. He should be your boss."

"Fuck you."

"You already said that one. Yeah, I bet that just pisses you off to no end. You're out bustin' your ass, puttin' your job on the line every day. And they don't trust you with this case. They bring in someone retired to get all the glory. And for what? So he could get shot in some basement?"

"You seem to have it all figured out."

"I do. I know you've been waitin' for somethin' like this. But I don't know why. Why do you hate him so much? It seems like he doesn't do anythin' but look out for you."

"Yeah, well fuck him and fuck you too. Now keep it the fuck down or I'll superglue your lips closed."

Oster shrugged. "Suit yourself."

Stanton stood in the dark alone. He turned the flashlight off and tucked it into his waistband. He pressed his left hand up against the wall, the firearm in his right. He walked slowly until he turned the corner past the metal table and was in what felt like a corridor. He stretched out his other hand and felt nothing.

"You still there, Jon?"

"Yeah, I'm here."

"Did you see that girl? She was damn fine, wasn't she?"

"She was," Stanton said, coming up with his firearm in front of him. "Where'd you find her?"

"She was just some whore, giving blow jobs to anyone that promised her she could be in a movie."

"You seem to have an affinity for those types of girls." Stanton walked across the corridor and measured five steps before he hit another wall. "Why them, Kyle?"

"'Cause they're whores, that's why. Not many people missed them, did they? The cops didn't seem to try too hard to find us."

Stanton felt around a corner. Bonnie's voice was louder now, echoing off the walls.

"Philip's outside. He brought us here."

"Philip's a fucking weasel. I should've killed him a long time ago."

"Why didn't you?"

"He'd been doing this a lot longer than me. I needed someone to show me around the block."

"So you found him?"

"Yeah, I hired him actually."

Stanton froze. "You hired him to kill your daughter?"

Silence a moment. "Damn, you are as good as that cunt at the DA's Office said you were." He chuckled. "She said if anyone could find out who did this to my daughter it was you. Guess she was right."

"Why would you do that?"

"I loved her. More than anyone could love someone. Since she was thirteen I was in love with her and didn't want to be with anyone else, and you know what she did? She ran away and started fucking on film for money. You believe that? A daughter of mine on film fucking for money?" He sighed. "Anyway, Philip showed me how much fun you could get out of life if you just let all that shit about morality and God and all of that go. You just let it go and you're suddenly free. In a second, you're a different person and the whole world's open to you."

"Submitting to the whim of all of our desires isn't freedom, Kyle. You traded morality to become a slave to everything that comes into your head. And a lot of innocent people were killed." Stanton came around another corner. He felt air on his face. An opening was somewhere nearby and he felt as if he was in open space rather than between walls.

"I wasn't as careful as I should've been. Next time'll be much better. It'll be easy actually. I'm planning on opening a casting agency. They'll just come to me, Jon. I'll put out an ad and they'll come alone to any address I want them to. That's what I should've done from the beginning."

Stanton took a few more steps. He could hear breathing not far away.

"Yeah," the voice said, "it's going to be better this time."

Stanton heard feet shuffling. Before he could move, something struck him on the side of the head with so much force it sent him off his feet. He hit the ground and heard his firearm slip away from him and tumble.

Stanton rolled as something impacted the ground next to him. His head throbbed and he felt the warmth of blood on his skin. He got to his knees before the next blow came. It was to his back and sent him face first into the ground. Another blow to the ribs, and the breath left his body. He rolled again and heard several more impacts against the ground where he had been. Bonnie couldn't see either.

Stanton lay perfectly still, and held his breath.

"You can't hide from me. There's no way out but past me. You hear me, Jon?"

The clink of metal on metal. Bonnie grunted as something hit the ground. He was thrusting with something blindly. Stanton moved and Bonnie was on him.

Stanton felt liquid fire enter his leg and knew he had been stabbed. He howled in pain and Bonnie laughed.

"See, you're just a visitor down here. But I live in the dark."

The knife in his leg twisted and Stanton rolled to his back. The pain rocketed up and down his body as the tip of the knife scraped bone.

More clinks of metal as Bonnie stabbed furiously at the ground. Stanton crawled to the side, reaching for a wall, but didn't feel anything. He stopped for a second and quietly let out his breath but Bonnie heard and lunged at him. Stanton twisted and kicked with his leg, hitting Bonnie in the face. He kicked again, nailing him in the chin before he tried to crawl away on his back.

Bonnie grabbed his legs and pulled him down, swinging with the knife. Stanton, instinctively, held up his forearms, blocking the blow. He could feel the tip of the knife scraping his cheek. He turned his head away from it as Bonnie put his weight down and the knife hit the ground.

Bonnie lifted it again and stuck it into Stanton's leg, nearly where the other wound was. Stanton screamed as Bonnie pinned him down, laughing.

"You should've left it alone," Bonnie said, withdrawing the knife. He bent down over Stanton, cradling him around the ribs. "Phil was going to take the fall and I would've eventually left the state. Everyone could've been happy."

Stanton could feel his arms move as he lifted the knife.

"But now, Jon, now you're going to die."

Stanton pulled out the flashlight. "You first."

He held it up to Bonnie's face and clicked it on. The sudden beam of light caused him to screech and turn away. A large Bowie knife was in his hand. Stanton dropped the flashlight and grabbed Bonnie's hand. He thrust it toward him with everything he had. He felt a warm spray over his face as Bonnie released a wet gurgle. Stanton gave it a final push and felt it tear through mounds of flesh.

Bonnie collapsed to the side, sucking in breath. Stanton grabbed his light. The knife had gone through his throat, the tip sticking out from the back of his neck.

Stanton scanned the room and saw his firearm. He crawled over, his leg useless, and picked it up. He leaned against the wall and held the weapon in one hand and the flashlight in the other, the muzzle aimed at Bonnie's face. He was flopping around, pulling at the knife but he pulled at an angle that just made the slick, wet flesh tear even more. Blood pooled around him, black in the light. It ran like a small stream over the uneven ground.

Bonnie stopped moving. Stanton began to crawl toward the hole, and to the young girl who he could still hear crying in the tunnel.

CHAPTER 48

Jon Stanton lay on the sand in Ocean Beach Park. The sun barreled its rays down. He felt hot after just a few minutes and had to put up an umbrella. He stood too quickly, forgetting about the stitches in his leg, and the wounds sent little shocks of pain to remind him. He glanced to Emma, who was in the shallow with her friend. She pointed down, meaning for him to sit down and not move, and he held up a finger indicating he would in a minute.

The umbrella had buckled previously in a windstorm, and he had to bend each metal bar to straighten it. It was then that he saw Stephen Gunn park and come onto the beach.

"Hey," Gunn said.

"Hey. Even to the beach you wear a leather jacket?"

"Well, it's my thing, you know. Is that your woman?"

Stanton looked back to Emma, who was now walking toward them. "That's her."

He shook his head. "Gotta hand it to you, man. This ain't a bad life you got here. So no police work again, huh?"

"No."

"Hm. You sure about that?" He hesitated. "All the media this got, they promoted me. I'm gonna be a captain of my own unit."

"I read that. Congratulations, Stephen."

"Thanks."

The two men looked at each other, both thinking the same thing but neither of them saying it.

"Anyway, Jon, if you ever wanted to come back. There would be a spot on my unit whenever. If there's not, I'll make room."

"What's the matter, Stephen? Don't believe the thugs you're going to surround yourself with are gonna be able to solve crimes?"

"What the fuck are you talkin' about?"

"You shouldn't be wearing a badge. Childs told me what you said. You wanted me to die in there, didn't you?"

"I didn't want anything like that—"

"Don't lie to my face."

Gunn stepped in close. "If I wanted you dead, I could do it anytime."

"I know you could." Gunn turned and began walking away. Stanton shouted, "Don't take the job, Stephen. It'll destroy you." He got into his car and slammed the door. "And everyone around you," Stanton whispered.

"What did he want?" Emma said, walking up behind him.

"I think he just wanted to say goodbye."

It was well into the afternoon and Stanton had just woken up from a nap. A cool breeze was blowing over the beach, and high-school kids that had just gotten out of school were beginning to take over, looking to get in a few hours before the waves died down. Stanton glanced over and saw Emma asleep next to him. Tonight, they would be catching a flight to Maui, and in the morning, Stanton was taking her by helicopter to the mouth of a volcano. He reached into his pocket and felt the velvet carrying case for the engagement ring he had purchased two days ago and had been too nervous to leave in his apartment.

He turned on his cell phone and saw that he had a text message: PLEASE CALL THIS NUMBER, URGENT. A second text held a phone number. It appeared to be an overseas number. Probably a scam. He'd received texts and emails saying similar things before, but just in case, he stood up, using the cane the hospital had provided, and limped far enough away that he wouldn't wake Emma.

He stood at the lip of the ocean and watched the waves roll

in as he dialed the number. A male voice answered.

"Is this Jon Stanton?"

Stanton's stomach dropped. His knees felt weak and he leaned heavily on his cane. "Eli?" he said, his voice hardly a whisper.

"Do you miss me? I miss you, believe it or not. I think about you far more than I thought I would."

"Where are you?" Stanton said, glancing around.

"Really, Jon? That's your master plan to get me to tell you where I am? Just ask me?"

"I hadn't exactly planned for this."

"Really? I don't believe you."

"What do you want?"

"You know there was a time when I could call you at two in the morning and you'd pick up and listen to whatever I had to say."

"We're not friends, Eli."

"Oh, I know. We both have the scars to attest to that. I just called to congratulate you."

"On what?" Stanton said, his mind racing. He wondered if there would be any way to trace the call after he'd hung up and if it would even matter. He had no doubt Eli would get rid of the phone after this call.

"On the Blum case. That was a tough one. I really didn't think you'd find him until he got arrested for something else."

"Why'd you let him go? Was it fun for you to see him out?"

"Let who go?"

"Philip Oster. You had a line on him and you didn't share it with me."

"Jon, I'm not sure what you're talking about." Stanton was silent. "Oh," Sherman chuckled, "is that how they got you to come back? They said we could've stopped him but I buried the leads? Oh, that is brutal. Guilt's a powerful emotion."

"Eli, I want you to turn yourself in. This has got to stop."

"No, I don't think so. I'm having too much fun. That was your problem, you know. Not enough fun. Your surfing was meditation for you but you always had a hard time turning that mind of yours off and just having fun. But they are hard to turn off, aren't they? Minds like ours."

"There is no *ours*."

"Don't delude yourself, Jon. You know why you were able to catch Kyle Bonnie? Because you think like him. You have urges like him. I know you have your deductions and mathematical models but that's not it, Jon. Deep down, you're just like them. That darkness. It's in you."

"We all have a choice. We can choose who we are and what we do." Stanton sat down, suppressing a groan of pain. "I want you to turn yourself in, Eli. Come home and turn yourself in. It's the only way you can find peace."

"Now how would my date tonight feel about that? She was planning for a fun night out on the town. I can't just abandon her." Stanton could hear people in the background and Sherman walking away from them.

It lasted only a moment, no more than a couple of words, but Stanton heard them: it was Chinese.

"What's the matter, Jon?"

"Don't kill her, Eli. Let her go."

"No. Unless you're willing to trade something."

"What?"

"I want you to murder someone, Jon."

"Eli—"

"You can pick anyone you want. Find some atrocious sex offender on the state list and go to their house and put a bullet in their head. That life for the young girl I'm taking out tonight. That's the only way."

"You would kill her anyway. Your urge is too strong. You can't control it any more than you can control your breathing."

He laughed. "See, I told you we're the same. It's not our fault either, Jon. We're monstrous beings in nature. We rape and kill and hunt whenever we like. And then we come into society and we're expected to just quell those urges. Quell a million years of evolution. It can't be done. So we get depressed and we turn into addicts and alcoholics and all the rest. But not me and you. Me and you, Jon, we know what we are. And that self-knowledge is what frees us. I'm curious, though; if you believed me, would you have done it?"

"Jon," Emma yelled out, "we gotta go, babe."

"Oh," Eli said, "now who is that?"

Stanton took a deep breath. "I'm going to kill you, Eli. There won't be a trial or an arrest. Some evils are too great to allow."

"I know. I've seen it, in my dreams. Me and you. It's not clear that you kill me though. Funny thing, isn't it? Anyway, I'll let you get back to your little woman. I know mine is getting antsy."

The line went dead. Stanton slipped the phone into his pocket and rose, walking back over to Emma.

"I'll have to meet you at the airport," he said.

"Why?"

"I have to make a quick stop."

The first call Stanton made was to the FBI's Criminal Apprehension Unit out of the Los Angeles office. He spoke with his old friend, Mickey, who had once been a police sergeant before being recruited into the bureau.

"You sure it was Chinese?" Mickey said. "Not Korean or Japanese?"

"Positive. I took two years of Mandarin in high school."

"Well, that narrows it down to about four or five countries. It's better than nothing. You know him best. If you ever want to help out with this, lemmie know."

Stanton parked outside the District Attorney's Office. "I don't think so, Mickey. But thanks."

He stepped out and went inside. Taking the elevators up, he felt anger flush inside of him and had to work to control it. Anger is the most destructive of all emotions because it drowns out all the others. Controlling it was something he'd had to work on since he was a child.

He stormed past the secretary who was shouting at him and into Kathleen Ackerman's office. She was going through documents and looked surprised to see him.

"You lied to me."

Kathleen looked to her secretary. "Call security please."

"Do you even care that I could've died?"

"Do you care how many girls that man would've killed, did kill, because we couldn't catch him?"

"So you sit with the killer in your office and lie to me?"

"It was..."

"It was what? At least have the guts to finish your sentences."

"It was his idea."

Stanton was silent a moment. "Why? Why did he want me on his daughter's case?"

"I don't know, Jon. You're the psychologist. You tell me."

Stanton looked at her a long time, until security arrived, and then said, "I'll show myself out."

He walked out of the building and to his car. He sat in the driver seat. Bonnie had selected him. He wanted to be caught. A fragment of humanity was left in him. He knew he couldn't control the darkness. He wanted to be stopped.

The sheer layers of the mind were too much to contemplate. Sometimes it seemed like the unconscious and the conscious had no idea what the other was doing. That we're beings bound to always be at war with ourselves. Maybe Sherman had been right about that.

Stanton pulled out the box and the ring in his pocket. The ring was the end to one war. Moving out of this state and leaving behind anything having to do with investigation was another. We choose the wars we fight, and Stanton knew there was no better fight than the one with our natural selves. The spirit and the flesh were always at odds, but he had to believe that peace was possible. He wasn't there yet, but one day, he knew he would be.

Stanton started the car and pulled away, heading to the airport and to a new life.

Made in the USA
Las Vegas, NV
23 August 2022

53857483R00132